Contents

Young Wolf In Love

By
Pius Kasan

Introduction

No one even knew that it was possible, but seeing is believing.

Usually werewolves meet their mates after they meet their wolves for the first time when they are 16 years old. What will happen when the young alpha meets his mate at the age of 6?

Alana is a small abused 5 year old, Elijah is a overprotective 6 year old alpha. They have a connection like no one has seen before.

What will happen if soulmates meet as such a young age?

Chapter 1

Hayden's POV

I was sitting in my office doing paperwork, lost in thought. I just found out this morning that my beautiful mate is pregnant. Suddenly my beta's voice broke through my mind "Alpha Mr. Micheals and his family just arrived"

I replied with a quick "Be right there" before shutting the mind link. I received Mr. Micheals request to transfer to my pack a few months ago. He was one of the best warriors in his previous pack so it shocked me that he wanted to transfer. My pack was one of the strongest packs so I put my confusion aside and decided to meet up and begin the tranfer process.

While walking down to meet the Micheals family something kept on bothering me about them. Although he is a great warrior, I did my research on them and they have transferred to 5 different packs in 3 years. Which is strange because wolfs are pack animals and don't usually like leaving their packs, they get protective and attached to the people in their pack.

When I made my way to them, I saw a bulky, strong scary looking guy. Well he would look scary to most people, but not high ranking pack members. He was standing next to a woman, I guess his mate, who had this evil look in her eyes. I gave my beta a quick glance and saw he had a very unimpressed look on his face.

Behind the couple on the steps was this beautiful little girl, I'm guessing she is about 3 years old, with long pitch black hair and strikingly blue eyes, a strange but yet perfect combination. Her skin was white, looking overall like the perfect porcelain doll.

My beta, Alex, finally spoke up "Alpha this is warrior Jakob and his *girl...*" Alex gave me a strange look while saying *girl* but continued "Ms Carla and behind them is their 5 year old Alana" my eyes widened a bit at the 5 year old part, but I quickly composed myself. She did not even look 4 years old, she was so tiny and fragile.

The Micheals gave me a quick nod and I signaled them to follow me back towards my office. We weren't even walking for a minute when I heard a 'oempf' behind me and turned to see little Lana tripped and fell. She quickly looked up and I saw her trying to keep her tears back.

I turned to see Mr. Micheals looking mad at her. Like smoke coming out of his ears mad. I did not understand this, why mad? at who? It was an accident why aren't they helping her up? I was about to go to her when I heard a little growl behind me.

Before I can even process what is happening there is another growl "mine" and a little tanned, brown haired ball, running past me to the girl pulling her to him and cradling her like she is the only thing that matters in the world.

It took me a few seconds to process what I'm seeing. If I wasn't seeing it with my own eyes I wouldn't believe it was true. I didn't even know it was possible.

But here right in front of my eyes is my 6 year old son cradling the beautiful little girl.

His mate.44

♡ ♡

Elijah's POV:

I am in a terrible mood today. Mommy asked if I woke up on the wrong side of the bed today. I didn't even know there was a wrong and a right side of the bed I just got out of bed to get ready for school. But I didn't tell her that, I just ignored her and went on with my day.

At school my best friend and future beta, Zander, wanted to play during lunch break, but I wasn't in the mood. We have been friends since I was born so he knew something was wrong with me today so he didn't bother me.

I don't know whats wrong with me either today, I didn't mean to be in a bad mood today. Something, a feeling in my mind just keeps bothering me today.

And now I also feel bad for ignoring my momma today because she packed my favourite cheese sandwich today for lunch AND she added an extra juice box. I **love** juice!

Momma and daddy calls me a juice junky but I don't care. Even alphas can drink juice, I see daddy drink juice most mornings with breakfast. And that yucky red stuff they say is made of grapes most nights with momma at dinner. But I tasted that and it does NOT taste like grape juice to ME! But they like this so called 'wine'. I'll stick to normal juice thank you.

The rest of the classes after lunch was just as boring as the ones before lunch. The only reason I still go to school is because daddy says I will need it to be a good alpha. And that it is a way to interact with my fellow pack members. I dont feel very interactive today.

After school my ghost like body drifts back to my daddy's office, I go there after school sometimes then he or his delta, Caleb, walk with me back home. I can see some of the pack pups playing around while walking back to the pack house, I don't bother with them too much today. Just a 'hello' or 'hey' every once in a while. Got to remember my manners.

While walking I spot my dad and his beta and some other people I don't recognize, and start making my way towards them.

When I get closer I spot the prettiest girl I've ever seen, and my mood is instantly better. She has this black hair that goes all the way to her bum. And even from meters away I can see her sky blue eyes. She looks so tiny, but she is the perfect size.

Suddenly she trips over a rock and falls. I instantly speed up to get to them quicker. As I get closer I smell the most amazing scent ever, vanilla like my favourite cake and strawberry like my favourite milkshake. I'm almost at the group of people and still no one is trying to help her up.

I can see that she is holding back some tears and I hear this small growl. It took me a second to realize the growl came from me, I've never made that sound before.

Rather than helping the pretty girl, the people just stood there. What is wrong with them? I growl another *'mine'* before I am right by her side in seconds. I'm sure I've never moved that fast.

I scoop her up and hold her tight in my arms. I feel her whimper and flinch a bit so I loosen my grip, but I don't let her go. I keep her cradled to me, and she starts to tighten her tiny arms around my waist.

After a few minutes I look up from her pretty face to see all the adults, even my daddy just staring at us. I growl at them and they look at each other shocked.

I look at the pretty girl in my arms and whisper to her "Hello pretty girl, my name is Elijah, your okay now. What's your name?" Her little angel voice reply me also in a whisper "Hey Lijah, my name is Alana"

I pull her a little closer to my body and mumble 'pretty' into her hair. Because she is definitely the prettiest angel on earth.

Elijah's POV:

I held little Lana as close as possible without hurting her. I looked up to the adults my eyes meeting the two strangers and they gave me a disgusted look?

I didn't let them bother me as I looked at my daddy with big pleading eyes en said "She's hurt, we *need* to help her"

He started walking towards us and a growl involuntarily escaped my lips. He held his hands up in surrender and told me "Son I can't help her if you don't allow me to come near her. I'm only going to help it's okay."

Hayden's POV:

Elijah nodded his head slowly, and I went closer and bent down in front of them. "Hello Lana, are you okay? Where are you hurt sweetie?" I said in a tiny voice not to scare her.

I can see the tears building up in her eyes again and Eli pulls her closer to calm her down. I've never seen anything like this before, but I'll comment on that later when both the little munchkins in-front of me is back to being happy kids.

I see Alana glance towards Mr. Micheals with big eyes and I looked at him too. He looks angry? tense? Something is not right.

Alana looks back towards me and whispers "I'm okay. I *will* be okay" like she is trying to convince herself more than me. While Eli gives me those big pleading eyes again.

I slowly lift my hand and brush a loose strand of hair out of Alana's face. I see her flinch slightly and I know something is definitely not right. She is not just shy, she is scared, terrified.

I mind link Alex "Take those two to my office, something is off, I have *bad* feeling about this. I'm taking the girl to the doctors so they can check her out."

"Glad I'm not the only one who got that feeling. I'll keep a close eye on the so called parentals, link me when you have news." Alex replies, as I see him explain something and lead them away.

I scoop Eli up in my arms with Alana still in his arms and start walking to the pack hospital. Alana whispers "what's happening" while Eli just runs his hand up and down her back whispering back "we are going to help you"

When we enter the pack hospital people are staring at us, wondering why I'm carrying the two pups this strange, semi on top of each other. But I don't let them bother me and neither does the pups.

As I round the corner to Dr. Martin's office my mate stares at me with wide, terrified eyes thinking something happened to her pup. I give her a small smile indicating everything is fine. And she starts walking with us with a confused expression on her beautiful face, with her full eyebrows scrunched together.

I walk into Dr. Martin's office and put the pups on the bed and the instantly cuddle closer to each other. I can see shock on both the doctor and my mate's face so I open a mind link between the three of us to explain to them that they are mates. Yes more shock from the two ladies in the room, and I can see tears forming in my mate's eyes so I pull to my side and hold her. Then I ask Dr. Martin to do a full checkup on Alana.

"Hey Alana..." Dr. Martin didn't get to say anything else or move closer because another growl left Eli's lips leaving the ladies stunned.

"Elijah Grey Stevens you do not growl at the docter" a chuckle escaped my lips at my mate's scolding while Eli had a guilty look on his face. She gave me the scary 'don't mess with me' mate look and I had to explain "Baby, she is definitely not the first person he's growled at today"

She gave me big eyes and whispered "he growls now?" Which just made me chuckle more. Yes I'm a big scary Alpha who chuckles when around his mate. With the mate bond a lot is possible.

Dr. Martin explained to the pup that she is just trying to help and has to check that Alana is okay. Eli refused to let Alana go so in the end the settled with holding hands to allow Dr. Martin to do her work.

When Dr. Martin is done with her checkup, Eli goes back to cuddling Alana while Dr. Martin comes over to talk to me and my mate.

"Alpha it is not good she has definitely been *abused*"

♡ ♡ ♡ ♡ ♡ ♡ ♡ ♡ ♡ ♡ ♡ ♡ ♡ ♡ ♡ ♡ ♡ ♡

Chapter 2

Lila's POV

"*Alpha she's definitely been abused*" Those words keep repeating in my mind as I look at my son holding the tiny pup in his arms.

From the look on her face she is very content on just staying there in his arms forever. Her eyes were starting to get heavy and she is going to fall asleep any second. I put a hand on my tummy, I won't ever let anything bad happen to my kids how can parents allow that.

I still can't believe my baby boy found his mate, he's only six. I am happy for him, but I was suppose to have ten more years of being the only woman in his life.

I look at my mate and see him trying to stay calm. He turns towards me and buries his head in my neck and inhales my scent to calm himself down. He whispers into my neck "Baby, you take the pups home and get them something to eat and ready for bed, I'll be right there, I just have to take care of her so called parents in my office". We've been mates for years and I still get that nice feeling in my tummy when he holds me close.

All I can do is nod. He gives me a peck on the lips and turn and leave. I turn to the pups to go get them to make our way home.

Hayden's POV:

People should be glad my mate was near me to calm me down a bit. That girl is so small and innocent.

I mind link Alex "Get 4 guards to my office and keep an eye on Mr. Micheals and his *girl* - That sweet girl has been abused. I'll be there in a sec" I don't even let him reply before I shut the mind link.

Not even a minute later I'm storming into my office, not even caring to look who else is inside, I walk straight up to Jacob Micheals and spit the word "explain".

Both his and Carla's faces turn into a sneer and he says "I don't need to explain anything to you!" I had to use all the strength I had to keep calm, and I can sense the same goes for my beta.

"It is against the law to hurt innocent wolves, so unless you want to die right here, right *now*. I'd explain if I were you" My voice came out calm and deadly. I can see Jacob's adam's apple blob from nerves.

"She was a mistake, the little brat was never even supposed to be born. I was supposed to have a son! A guy like me deserves a strong son who would be the perfect warrior. All the little bitch wants to do is play in the garden!"

I open my mouth to speak but Jocob just continues "Her mother was happy she gave birth to a daughter, how can someone be happy to give birth to a little 'good for nothing' so I got rid of her and got me a woman who wants a boy, a woman who wants a child that would change the world!"15

I looked at him and his 'woman' with disgust. I can't believe he just said that about his own daughter. And he killed his own mate? How can someone even do that?34

I turned towards my beta "Get them to sign over there guardian duties, there is no way I'm ever letting them near little Lana ever again and take them to the cells. I'll start the paperwork to send them to the blood moon prison in the morning"

"NO!!" I turn back to look at the two screaming people behind me, who is being held in place by my guards. "I am an asset to your pack! I am a great warrior! You can't send us to the blood moon prison. That is the worst prison out there for werewolf kind"

"If your such a great warrior I'm sure you'll survive between those blood thirsty werewolves we put there. Because it is exactly where you belong." With that said I left my office and went back home.

As soon as I got home and opened the door I heard screaming coming from upstairs "NO!!" And I made my way upstairs as fast as I could, every possibility of things that could have gone wrong running through my brain.

Alana's POV:

I've never felt loved or safe ever in my life before. As long as I remember I've been called a 'mistake'. Mr. Micheals, yes I had to call my own father Mr. Micheals, and Carla always said I was never supposed to be born.

They said I'm not strong and that I'm a brat. I am not even allowed to have fun I only went out to play in the garden when I knew they were away or they didn't know I was outside. I **love** gardens, flowers and butterflies.

The only other fun thing I did was read. I had a few books the pupsitters gave me that I hid in my room. Otherwise I have to clean up the messes they make. Take their things to their room, wash the floors. I get thrown around and Mr. Micheals hits me with his belt on my back if he is mad, drunk, in a bad mood or just feels like it.

Everytime someone at a pack got suspicious of how I was treated we would move to a different pack. They kept telling me 'we are just keeping your worthless ass around until Carla gets pregnant and we have a perfect boy, then we're dropping you off somewhere in the woods'.

I was not happy with the move to 'Alpha Hayden's' pack. I had a secret friend in my old pack. And when I tripped over that stupid rock, the beating from two days ago hurt so bad, and I knew I'd be in trouble for 'making a scene'.

So when I heard the little growl and I was suddenly pulled into a hug, I had so many emotions. First pain, confusion and then, strangely warmth, love and safety. I didn't know what love and safety was but I'm sure that is what it should feel like. And I never *ever* want to let go of it again.

But of course the lady in the long white coat said I **had** to. So Lijah said he will let go of my body, but he won't let go of my hand. But as soon as the crazy lady was done sticking things in my mouth and looking at things on my skin and listening through weird things, I cuddled back into Lijah's warmth and safety.

After a while Alpha HayHay left, I wasn't scared of him so much anymore because Lijah said it's his daddy, and he is helping us be safe.

Eventually we went home with Lijah's momma, she didn't say much she just kept looking at us. When we got to the house I had to work hard not to run up and smell all the pretty flowers. The garden was so big and pretty. I wonder if I will be allowed to play in this garden.

Lijah's momma made us some chicken strips to eat for dinner, I've never had those. I wasn't allowed to eat a lot before, they said me eating was a waste of their money. I don't even know what money is.

I was sitting on Lijah's lap, and he was waiting for me to take the first piece of chicken. But it burnt my fingers so I pulled back quickly and put my fingers in my mouth. Lijah gave a big gasp while his momma kept saying 'sorry'. So for the rest of the dinner Lijah made sure the chicken was cold enough so I won't burn and he was feeding me between bites of his own.

When it came to bath time to get ready for bed neither me nor Lijah was very happy because his momma said we had to let go of each other, **completely!** After a few minutes of arguing between Lijah and his momma and some threats about taking his juice away? And her promising it is only for a few minutes we separated to our own bathrooms.[17]

Lijah's momma introduced herself as Lila and she helped me get a bath ready with some nice bubbles. She gave me all these nice scented soapies and she helped me wash my hair while I popped the bubbles.

She gave me some of Lijah's clothes I could wear and told me that she will get me some girl clothes in the morning, but I didn't care to wear his clothes because it smells nice like him.

After the nice hot bath it was time for bed. And a whole new argument started because they wanted us to sleep in different rooms?

I am not leaving Lijah for a whole night. We were clinging to each other and the argument got a bit loud and before I knew it a loud 'NO!' escaped my lips.

Next thing I know Alpha HayHay is in the room with us looking at us with big eyes and tears were falling down my cheeks.

Hayden's POV:

"What is going on in here?" Everyone suddenly went quiet and turned towards me. My mate and son both looked furious while little Lana has tears streaming down her face. Now I wish I didn't come home so soon maybe I would have missed the drama.

"I..I'm so..sorry. I didn't mean to.. to make trouble" the little girl gets out between tears and hiccups. While Eli pulls her closer to him and gives his mom 'the mad look'.

I quickly bend down infront of her en softly tell her "it's okay sweetie, you're not in trouble. Lila and I are going outside to talk, we'll be back in a few minutes". With that said I stood back up and led my mate outside.

"What happened baby?" I can see the frustrated look on her face and I take her hand in my own and rub circles on her knuckles.

"Uhg... I don't want to be the bad guy, but I told them they can't sleep in the same room and they lost it. I really didn't think our mate, relationship, sleepover whatever you want to call it speech would be given this soon."

I just keep rubbing her knuckles while she ramble. "He is our baby boy, why does he have to grow up so fast. And they were apart for bathtime and she seemed fine but the refuse to leave each other alone. He was even feeding her, our six year old baby. I'm not ready for the mate speech."

When she is done with her rambling she falls into my embrace and I just hold her for a few seconds until she feels better, thinking about everything she said... Mate speech? Feeding her?

"Baby they are going to be fine, everything is going to be fine. We are going to take it day by day. We can give them the speech tomorrow? As for tonight we can make some compromises for them on the sleeping arrangements and then figure everything out tomorrow, it's getting late. And he will always be your baby boy. Alana seems like a nice girl." I pull her back to me and give her a kiss on the forehead.

"I love you, baby. Now come on let's go figure out the sleeping arrangements." With that said I gently pull her back to the room and open the door.

With the light coming from the hallway shining onto the bed we can see the two pups already in bed cuddled up and asleep.

They are both semi facing each other, little Lana has her head on Eli's shoulder chest area. Eli has his arms wrapped tightly around her small body, like if he let's go of her she might disappear. Eli's head is buried deep inside her long black hair.

I look to the side to see my mate with an involuntary smile on her face, deep in thought. I leave the room quickly to go get a juice box to put on Eli's nightstand like we do every night just in case he gets thirsty.

When I get back to the room I see my mate standing next to the bed leaning over and giving both the pups goodnight kisses on the forehead. I put the juice box down and do the same and lead my mate quietly out of the room.

Always give your kids goodnight kisses it doesn't matter if they are awake or asleep.

With that we get ready for bed ourselves with everything that happened during the day going through our minds. And thinking of what the future holds for everyone.

♡ +

Wow finally the end of the day!

Chapter 3

Elijah's POV

Last night after mommy and daddy left the room to go 'talk', I could see my little girl getting tired but the tears just kept coming out of her eyes and she kept saying 'sorry'.

I gently pulled her to the bed and pulled the covers back "Let's get into bed baby girl, no one is mad at you. You don't have to be sorry."

She nodded and got into bed. I got in next to her, I pulled her comfortably close to me "go to sleep baby girl" she just nodded and mumbled a 'goodnight'

I gave her a goodnight kiss on the forehead. I didn't want to fall asleep I just wanted to hold her and protect her, but my eyes got sooo heavy.

When I woke up I was so happy she was still in my arms. A little more on top of me than last night but still in my arms so I don't care. She looks so peaceful in her sleep.

I'm trying to move as little as possible not to wake her, but then I spot my favorite juice next to me. I'm so thirsty. No, I don't need to drink that juice right now.

After a few more minutes of just staring at the pretty girl in my arms she begins to stir and wake up. I don't know if I'm happy or sad, I'm still going to hold her when she is awake, just probably not so close.

No, I'm definitely happy she is awake, now I can look into those perfect blue eyes, that makes me feel like I'm swimming in happiness. She mumbles a "Good morning Lijah, I'm thirsty"

Thirsty... I can help with that. Without thinking twice I take my juice box from the table open it up and give it to her. After a few seconds I realized I just gave her my *favorite* juice. I *never* share my juice with *anyone.*

I didn't even realize but I must have looked at the juice longingly, because next thing I know she turns the juice box and pops the straw in my mouth. I take a long big sip. I have *never* been this happy in my life. I will always share my juice box with her and *only* her.

Then I realize mommy and daddy is at the door looking at us. They make us get up and 'ready for the day' because they need to 'talk' to us. Luckily we don't have school today because it's a Saturday.

After we are dressed we make our way downstairs for breakfast. I eat as slow as possible because I'm not ready for 'the talk', but of course they tell me to hurry up.

So now we are sitting in the livingroom, mommy and daddy in front of us and my little girl in my arms. Mommy is the first to start speaking "Babies do you know what mates are?" I reply without a doubt "Yes, it's our soulmate, the love of your life, your other half"

"You are right son, we want to talk to you today because you and Alana are mates" I look at my baby girl and my heart instantly swells. "No one has ever found their mates this soon so it is new for all of us so we are going to have to make some rules"

My face drops at the 'rules' part. I hate following rules, I'm the future Alpha, I make rules I don't follow them. But I see Lana shyly nod, so I listen. *Rules?*

"Okay, so we know you don't want to let each other go" I look at Lana and pull her closer to me, I can already feel that I am *not* going to like this rule. "But you are going to have to let go of each other sometimes" Yep, I was right, I do not like this rule.

"Son you still have to spend time with your friends, and little Lana has to make other friends too" Other friends? What is wrong with daddy, she does *not* need other friends. "You still have to have your weekly sleepover with your friends" That's a nice rule those are FUN! Little Lana can join, she is also my friend now.

"And then living and school arrangements. Little Lana you will never have to live with those terrible people again, okay?" I see tears in her eyes and she nods while mumbling 'thank you'. "Lila and I were talking and we are finding you a nice home..."-*finding?* "She can stay here"

"No son, she can't stay here. She can visit a lot but she can't stay here. We spoke to Caleb and his mate, they live right next door, they don't have pups yet and they will let her live with them." Caleb? The Delta? They are nice, but I want her to stay here.

"We are not arguing about this son. It's final they are excited and the already started making her a pretty room. You can visit a lot, it is close and it is for the best." Can he *always* read my mind? I look at my little angel, and although she looks stressed she looks willing to try so I nod at my dad to continue, but I do not wipe the angry look off my face.

"Now for school, we already enrolled her so she can start on Monday." I look at my dad suspiciously there is something he is not telling me. "She will be in *my* class?"

He just sighs "No son, she can't be in your class she is younger" Now I am definitely angry. "No! She has to be in my class! She is smart she can do it, I will help her. If she is not in my class I am never going back to school."

My parents glance towards each other and slowly nod "Okay, we will see what we can do, if she is smart enough she can be in your class." I look at my angel and see a nervous look on her face so I whisper "Don't worry you are smart enough. And I will help you. Always" I hug her closer and she relaxes and nods.

"Now get ready the boys are on their way for the sleepover, it is here tonight"

I think this is my longest chapter yet! What do you think about the *'rules'*?

Alana's POV:[1]

He wants me to go to big school with him? What if I'm not good enough? Will he be unhappy with me? I just want to make him happy he is so nice. I've always liked reading and the pupsitters in my previous pack said I was really smart. I just don't know about big school math![29]

But Lijah said he would help me and he looks smart so I might be fine. And I've never heard of this Caleb person or his mate but Lijah won't let me live with horrible people, I trust him.

I'm not sure I understand the whole mate thing yet? But Lijah seems to understand it, I guess that's all that matters. Loud noises at the door brought me out of my thoughts.

Next thing I know five very loud, hyperactive boys came running into the livingroom where we sat. Lijah stood up and happily gave each boy a bro hug then he quickly waved at the adults at the door and turned back to me taking my hand back in his own and smiling at his friends.

"Guys this is Alana, my mate" he looked back at me with a million dollar smile "Baby girl this is my best friends, Zander, my future beta" a boy with black hair and grey eyes nodded at me. "And then there is the twins, Aiden and Aaron. They are the Gamma's children." Two identical looking boys with blond hair and blue eyes gave me big smiles and waved.

"This is Charlie, my cousin, but everyone calls him Chubbs" I looked towards 'Chubbs' who gave me a mocking salute, he was a bit overweight compared to the other boys, with brown hair and eyes. He was definitely the 'clown' of the group. "And lastly this is Sammy, he is one of the Omega's sons" a Omega is the lowest rank in the pack but it didn't seem to bother these boys, you could see they love their friend no matter what. He was smaller then the other boys with light brown hair and eyes, and he had this cute dimple when he smiled at me.

I shyly waved at them, they all seem really nice. They decided that we are all going to the nearby swimming hole for the evening since the weather is great outside. The twins said I can borrow their sister's swimwear. And Chubbs went to grab a picnic basket his mom packed for the trip while Zander got towels and blankets.

The walk to the hole wasn't that long and the boys kept making jokes and playing all the way there while Lijah and I walked hand in hand.

Once we got to the swimming hole I was amazed, it was so beautiful! There was a waterfall, and the water was cleaner than I thought it would be. Chubbs was the first in the water with a big splash followed by the twins and Sammy, while Zander just rolled his eyes.

It looked really fun so I started removing my clothes I had on over the swimwear to get in as well, when I heard a growl behind me. I turned around to see all the boys with their back turned to me and Lijah smiling innocently at me.

We all got in. We played and splashed each other with water for what felt like hours until Chubbs got hungry and I got cold. So we had a picnic with sandwiches and drinks and lots of sweets before we made our way back home before it gets dark out. *Home*. I already think of this place as home. My so called parents long forgotten.

When we got back home all the adults were outside laughing and having fun of their own. We went inside, put on some dry clothes and made ourselves comfortable in front of the tv.

Well that was until the argument started on what to watch. I wanted to watch Frozen while Chubbs and the twins wanted to watch Spiderman. Lijah chose Frozen as well to which the boys looked shocked because apparently he loved Spiderman. Sammy also said he would watch Frozen which left the final decision up to Zander.

Apparently Lijah wasn't allowed to use the 'future alpha' card on his friends to get them to do something he wants, so instead he promised Zander cake to choose Frozen. Leaving Chubbs and the twins very disgusted when he agreed.

Aunty Li brought us more snacks just after the movie started. And I'm sure Chubbs ate half of them all by himself. Lijah and I were cuddled up on one couch, Sammy and Aiden on the other and the rest of the boys was on a mattress on the ground.

At some parts in the movie I was laughing my butt off *'watch out for my butt'...'it's so cute, it's like a little baby unicorn'...'I can't feel my legs'...* Olaf is the BEST!

I was getting really sleepy during the movie so with one last thought I drifted off to lala land...

'I love warm hugs'

Alana's POV:2

Today is the day I meet Caleb and his mate and move into their house. And to say I am scared would be putting it lightly. What if they don't like me? What if I do something wrong? I'm a little ter-rified. From now on I am going to be Lijah's neighbor. Will we still see each other a lot?

I put on some clothes Aunty Li gave me and slowly made my way downstairs. The first time Lijah's parents heard me call them Alpha HayHay and Aunty Li, their eyes grew big and I thought I did something wrong, I couldn't move. Until they both let out a big 'aww' and pulled me into a hug. I've never gotten much hugs so this all was very new to me, but I love it!

Hugs are now my favorite.

When I got outside where they were all waiting for me to walk next door together Lijah pulled me to his side and started walking while whispering "I'm here for you, *always*" which made me relax. He will always be there for me.

I didn't even notice we were at the door when it suddenly opened. A tall, big, muscled guy stood there. He had shoulder length blond hair, and the top half is pulled into a bun. If it wasn't for the smile ons his face and Lijah holding me I would have ran away. The man held onto a short, small lady with long braided brown hair.

At least they look friendly.

The man bent down but he was still taller than me "Hey ladybug, my name is Caleb and this is my mate Sophia." I blushed and smiled at the same time and whispered "I love ladybugs"

He gave me a big smile and reached out to pick me up. Just as he touched me Lijah growled, we all turned to look at him while his momma hit him on the back of the head "What did I say about growling at people?"

Caleb just started laughing and continued to pick me up while Lijah mumbled 'sorry'. "Let's show you where your room would be, when Sophia heard you were coming to stay here she went out and bought you a few things"

He walked with me on his hip upstairs, put me down infront of a closed door and gestured for me to go in. As soon as I opened the door I gasped and tears filled my eyes, it was *beautiful!*

It had lots of pink and teddies and toys, I had my own desk with coloring books and pens and everything I will ever need and never had. I had my own book case filled with books and a nice reading couch. It was just *perfect!*

My whole life all I could remember being in my room was my bed which was a terrible brown colour, an old dresser and the books I hid under my bed. I've never even had a teddy.

My tears wouldn't stop flowing. And they were mistaken for sad tears, Lijah and his parents were arguing about me moving back to their house when someone bend down next to me.

"Oo sweetie, don't cry, everything you don't like we can change, I knew I should have gotten princesses, girls love princesses. Now I'm starting to see it, it's all wrong, we could change..." I cut her off surprising myself and her a bit by giving her a big hug and crying into her shoulder.

The whole room got quite and I whispered "It's perfect, so perfect. I love it so much. Thank you, thank you, thank you." She held me tight in her arms and I can feel she also started crying and whispered back "You're so very welcome."

Caleb's POV:

Everything about this sweet girl came as a shock to all of us. When Hayden told us about her and asked Sophia and I if we would let her come live with us, we didn't hesitate to say yes.

Sophia and I have been trying to have pups for years, but something always went wrong and it resulted in miscarriages. We've gone to the doctor and he's always said he can't see a problem. But everytime she miscarriages I can see and feel a piece of our happiness breaking away forever.

After Hayden came to talk to us Sophia was over the moon. She immediately insisted I take her shopping so we can buy the little girl everything she will need and more, she don't want to get anything wrong because Hayden said they were not very happy with the move because she is afraid to leave Eli, she wants to stay with him.

I think Sophia went a bit overboard with the room, we don't even know what the girl likes yet, but I couldn't say anything, she was so *happy*.

The morning before they arrived she was so nervous she dressed and re-dressed what felt like a million times. She made us get up at 4am, like they weren't going to come way past 7am. Still *no* complaining just saying. She got ready and like expected we were way to early for them so she settled with walking up and down and staring out the window like a creeper to see if she can see them coming.[8]

When she finally saw them, I had to hold her tight in my arms to make sure she didn't get overexcited and scare the poor girl off. She looked so shy, but when I called her ladybug and she smiled my whole world turned upside down, she loves ladybugs. Oo man, she is going to have me wrapped around her small little pinkie.[5]

So when I picked her up one thought crossed my mind 'maybe I should be the one being held back not my mate' I did not realize how much I want this little girl in our lives and how excited I was.[1]

No! When she started crying when she saw her room, I thought my heart stopped right then and there. We just got her, we can't lose her now. Everything zoned out until I saw her hugging my mate. I could finally breath again.[2]

Hayden and his family left us alone so we can get to know the little ladybug, after a lot of convincing to Eli that she will be fine.

We were all sitting in her room just talking while she were playing with her bunny. There were a few more tears shed. But my new favourite sound in the word is definitely my ladybug and mate's joined laughter.[21]

My new *family*.

♡ ♡ ♡ ♡ ♡ ♡ ♡ ♡ ♡ ♡ ♡ ♡ ♡ ♡ ♡ ♡ ♡ ♡ ♡ ♡

Chapter 4

Alana's POV:

Today is my sixth birthday! I am so excited. Mommy and daddy is throwing me a big birthday party. Yes, I started calling Caleb and Sophia, mommy and daddy a few months after moving in with them. The first time it just accidentally slipped out.

Caleb was tickling me and I didn't even realize I said 'daddy stop!' He abruptly stopped and that's when I realized what I said but he looked so happy so I just continued calling him daddy and I saw that it bothered Sophia when I only called Caleb daddy so I started calling her mommy too. The first time she cried, she can be very emotional sometimes.

Back to my party. Mommy and daddy said a special girl like me deserves a special party. The invited *everyone. I've* made some friends of my own, and Lijah and the boys allow us all to join their sleepovers. I quickly got tired of it always just being me and the boys.

The first friend I made was Mila, she is the twin's sister, she is the only friend my own age since I'm in a class full of older pups. Nina, and Jessie are my other friends, they are both in my class, and they are sooo nice.

Besides our weekly sleepovers, are Lijah and I almost always at each others houses, he is still my bestest friend. He convinced/ blackmailed Alpha HayHay to build a little bridge to connect our windows so now visiting is even easier.

When I got outside I saw people already started arriving. There were balloons everywhere and a bouncy house and everything. Just as I saw Lijah walking up to me I felt someone tap my shoulder.

I turned to see Dan, he was a new boy in our class. Lijah *really* did **not** like him, I don't know why because he has always been nice to me. "Happy birthday Alana, I got this for you" I look down to see him holding a present with a nice big bow. Just as I was about to take it and thank him someone tackles him to the ground accidentally knocking me down in the prosses.

Tears fill my eyes as I see blood flowing out of my hand I landed on. "Lijah! Stop. What are you doing?" Zander pulls him off of Dan while my daddy pulls me up. That's when he realizes that I fell as well.

Now tears are freely flowing down my face and I can see regret in in Lijah's eyes, but he ruined my party, and he knew how excited I was for this party. It's my first birthday party ever.

My daddy takes me inside to bandage my hand and help me wash up, he tries to cheer me up by saying "it's not a party if something unplanned or unexpected doesn't happen" but it's definitely not making me feel any better.

"Why? Why would he do that?" He looks deep into my eyes wiping my tears away "I don't know ladybug, your going to have to ask him. Maybe he got a little jealous? It could be a mate bond thing. He would not have hurt you intentionally."

"Stupid mate bond" the words slip out of my mouth, and as soon as I said them I hear something fall at the door "You don't want to be my mate anymore?" I can see the regret in his eyes and how he is

30

struggling to keep his own tears from falling.

"I'll leave you pups to talk for awile" my daddy says, and he makes his way outside. "It was an accident, I didn't mean to get mad. I just wanted to give you my present first. And you know I don't like Dan, he is always extra friendly with you, and he has lots of friends he doesn't need you too, you're mine."

"I understand if you don't want to be my mate anymore, I'm sorry I didn't mean to ruin your party and hurt you" I look up from my bandaged hand and whisper "I still want to be your mate"

He release a big breath he was holding and pull my into a hug whispering 'I'm sorry' I push him away from me "And no more tackling people mister, I know aunty Li said no growling, but I much more prefer you going around growling at people than tackling people"

He gives me a misheavious smile and pulls me into another hug and whispers "I love you, baby girl" I instantly relaxes in his embrace and whisper back "I love you too Lijah" before pushing him back yet again.

"Now what is this tackle worthy present I just had to have first?" I say with a big smile on my face, everything long forgiven and forgotten.

His eyes turn big as he look back to where he dropped it when he entered. He quickly run back to get it and hand it over with a big smile. I open it and I gasp "Lijah, it's beautiful, I love it! Thank you, thank you, thank you! I'm never taking it off."

I gently swipe my fingers over the pretty butterfly necklace, it is the perfect gift!

My mommy comes into the house and tells me that most people have arrived, including all my friends. And are waiting outside for 'the birthday girl'. Yes, I pulled the 'you ruined my birthday card', while barely any people have arrived yet.

For the rest of the party I stick to my friends and Lijah and the boys. I did not see Dan again.

When it was time to blow out the candles and everyone sang 'happy birthday' my heart felt complete. I had the perfect family and the perfect friends. I have grown so much since I moved to this pack.

And the whole time while people sang 'happy birthday' my mommy was crying her eyes out saying "she's growing up so fast".

Alana's POV:

Lijah has been acting strange all day. Months have passed after my birthday and so far everything has been great, back to normal. But since I saw him this morning I knew something was off.

We walked to school together, but unlike normally he said nothing, just held my hand. And it's been like that the whole school day.

During lunch break, I asked him "penny for your thoughts" because that's what mommy usually tell daddy when he looks deep in thought, and then he tells her any and everything on his mind, so I thought it might work.

But I just heard him silently say after a few seconds "Do you have a penny?" And my face turned into a frown in disgust, I didn't know you had to have a penny, mommy never gives a penny. So I just mumbled a 'No' and looked down.

After a few seconds I looked back up, "But I do have one last cookie left" but he just shook his head, but before I can retrieve the cookie Chubbs grabs it and pops the whole thing in his mouth. I give him, or rather my cookie, a big eye longing look. "I ..ought u dint wan it" he says with a mouth full of cookie.

After school Lijah went straight home saying he had to do homework. I know his lying because we always do homework together after school, but I didn't say anything. I know he is hiding something from me, I just want to know what? He usually tells my everything.

So I had to do my homework all *alone*. And afterwards I went to play in the gardens. Not much playing in the garden if you ask me more like sitting on the grass poking my fingers in the ground. When Lijah is in a bad mood it makes me feel in a bad mood.

I've been sitting there for a few minutes when I saw Lijah walking to me with a determined look on his face so I jumped up with a big smile. He walked up to me but didn't stop. He kissed me on. the. lips.

He has kissed me before, but *never* on the lips. Usually it's on the forehead. I just stood there, eyes big. He had an equally shocked look on his face, so he just turns around and runs back to his own house.

I don't know for how long I stood there, frozen in my spot.

Elijah's POV:

Ever since yesterday I couldn't get what the bigger high school kids said out of my mind.

I went to the pack house to see my daddy. Momma sent me to get him because apparently it's his turn to give my baby sister, Belle, a bath.

But when I got to the pack house I bumped into some of the high school kids. They usually had something mean to say about me and Lana. Daddy says to just ignore them because they just do it because they're jealous that I already found my mate and they haven't.

This time they kept saying me and Lana aren't real mates because we don't kiss on the lips like real mates do. One of the older kids even kissed his mate to show me.

I just walked away and acted like they don't bother me, but it did bother me. Were they right? Were mates supposed to kiss on the lips?

So the whole next day, I couldn't get the thought out of my mind. I couldn't focus on anything else. I could see my little angel knew something was wrong and it was bothering her, but she didn't push me too much to tell her what is going on.

So after school I went home and put together all the courage I could and just walked up to her and kissed her on the lips. Her lips was so soft.

I saw her eyes get big, and my eyes got big, and all the courage I had before slipped away so I ran home as fast as I could. Why would I listen to those stupid, stupid high school kids?

Stupid, stupid, stupid.

What if she never look me in the eyes again? During the rest of the day, she came knocking on my window a few times but I couldn't open it.

My momma came to my room asking if everything was okay, but I just told her that I'm tired. Of course she went all overprotective mom on me, and had to do a whole temperature check and what felt like a whole doctor's checkup so she was sure I wasn't getting sick.

Late that night when I was sitting in bed, I heard another knock on my window. I held my breath hoping she'll go away and then I heard her saying "You can't hide from your mate forever" and I knew she was right, so I got up and opened the window.

I got back into bed and she got in next to me, quietly, not saying anything. So I started telling her everything that happened yesterday at the pack house with the high school kids.

By the end of my story she was laughing so hard tears were streaming down her cheeks. "You.. you listened to.. to the high school kids" she said between her laughter. "They always say the stupidest things, why listen to them, you kissed me, you kissed me." She said still laughing her little butt of.

"You kissed me back I felt your lips move." Saying that made her stop the laughing and her cheeks turning crimson. "We are never kissing again" *Never?* She can't mean that.

"Was it that bad? I'll be better at it when I'm older! I promise." With that another laugh escaped her lips. "I know, I mean not until we are big. But I am very happy you are my first kiss."

I am so happy she was my first kiss two, I felt her kiss my cheek and laying her head on my chest. I kissed the top of her head and decided that is the way I will kiss her until we are bigger.

With her in my arms, I peacefully fell asleep. She is my mate and we have all the time in the world to figure out how to be mates. I am not listening to those stupid high school kids again.

Aww, their first kiss.

Alana's POV:

I lie in bed with tears streaming down my face, what is going to happen to me now? Today is the worst day ever!

It started off good. Even though Lijah and his family went to visit a different pack this morning, I was okay. I went and played at Mila's house, I played in the garden. I was too busy to miss Lijah.

Because Alpha HayHay is gone for the day, daddy was extra busy with pack work, he didn't come home until dinner and that is when everything went all wrong.

Caleb's POV:

Today is the best day ever! No matter how much work I have to do, or what crosses my path. Nothing can wipe this smile off my face.

Throughout the day some pack members asked about my happy mood, while others teased me. But I'm keeping my mouth shut until we can tell my ladybug the great news.

At dinner my mate had everything set up to tell little ladybug, even some cupcakes to celebrate.

I could see her eyeing us suspiciously about our happy mood but she didn't say anything. Typical Lana, would never say or do anything to ruin someone's good mood.

After dinner it was time to tell her the good news. I took her hand in mine and with a big smile I spoke "Ladybug, Sophia is pregnant, we're having a baby."

I can see tears forming in her eyes "You're having a baby of your own?" I gently smiled "Yes we are, you're going..." before I could finish my sentence she was running off to her room.

I turned in confusion to my mate "Not happy tears?" She looks at me like I'm dumb "Did they look like happy tears to you?"

"We have been trying so hard for a baby, why isn't she happy? She is always happy about everything, she loves babies, she loves Belle. Why was she sad?"

I pulled my mate into my arms and hold her in my arms, and with my werewolf hearing I can hear my little girl's sniffles coming from upstairs. Great I'm in a house full of crying women. *Baby you better be a boy, daddy needs backup!*

When I finally got my mate to calm down and peacefully sleeping in bed I made my way to my little girls room. I stopped outside the door to listen, but all I could hear was some shuffling and sniffles. *Goody she is still awake.*

I made my way inside to see her crying and packing a bag? "Ladybug what are you doing? Why are you crying?"

"I love you, and I don't want to leave. Where am I supposed to go?" She looks up at me pleadingly through teary eyes. Leaving? "Why are you leaving baby girl?"

"You're having a baby of your own, you don't want me anymore." So *that* is what this is about! I start unpacking her bag while she just stares at me. Where does this crazy 6 year old girl think she is going this time at night?

"You're not going anywhere ladybug." She looks up at me with big eyes "I'm not?" I pick her up, take her to the bathroom to wash the tears off her face and get her ready for bed. *So much for eating celebratory cupcakes *sigh* women.*

I sit with her on the bed rubbing her tummy soothingly. "No you're not going anywhere, your going to live here with us until you're big enough to live in a house of your own." She looks up at me "But you're having a baby of your own"

"You are our baby too, which means your having a little brother or sister of you own too, just like Eli." Her face light up in excitement, and then immediately turned to disgust. Disgust? What is up with the women tonight.

"Lijah said after Belle was born she cried a lot and left stinky poops. Will my little brother or sister be like that?" A laugh escaped my lips "probably ladybug" and she looked at me with a cute scrunched up face.

"Go to sleep ladybug, Eli is coming back tomorrow" I said kissing her on the forehead, I know talking about the little man would lift her mood up, and looking at her face, it definitely did. It is still strange for me to think about my six year old daughter already having a mate. But it is amazing to see how they treat each other. They put some of the grown up mates to shame, showing them how to be proper mates.

Before I could stand up from her bed she grabbed my arm "Daddy where does babies come from" I looked at her with big eyes, choking on air. *Where does babies come from?*

I remember saying something about bunnies and flowers and maybe bees? And made my way out of the room before I could embarrass myself more. Yes, I definitely confused her more, and I'm hearing about it again tomorrow, I already know it.

And I was right. The next morning when I walked into the kitchen I saw my mate making breakfast and suddenly my ladybug asked "Mommy, where does babies come from? I asked daddy and he said something about bees and flowers and bunnies and gardens? I don't understand"

Gardens? What did I say to the poor pup? My mate looked at me with big eyes while I gave her a guilty look. No point in trying to deny it now.

"When two people love each other, and they are ready to be a mommy and daddy, there is a wizard that gives them a magic seed that the mommy takes and then the baby grows in her tummy." I look at my mate in amazement. *And all I could come up with is gardens, bunnies, bees and flowers?*

My little ladybug gets up and round the corner to look at my mates tummy "Hello baby" she says patting her tummy.

I get a mind link telling me that Alpha and his family is back. As soon as I tell Lana her face lights up like a Christmas tree, and she takes off running towards the door, me and Sophia following close behind.

She runs up to Eli jumping into his arms, with her little arms wrapped around his neck, and her short legs wrapping around his waist. If it wasn't for Hayden helping Eli to stay on his feet, he would have went flying backwards falling straight to the ground.

"I'm going to be a big sissy" I hear her telling Eli excitedly. He was not even gone for two days and she is not letting him go. I pity him when they are older and fully mated, when he needs to leave her for alpha meetings.

But he looks very comfortable with her wrapped in his arms.

♡ ♡ ♡ ♡ ♡ ♡ ♡ ♡ ♡ ♡ ♡ ♡ ♡ ♡ ♡ ♡ ♡ ♡ ♡

Chapter 5

3 year time jump!
Elijah 10 years & Alana 9 years.

Alana's POV:

Another pack's Alpha is visiting our pack today. He wants to talk to Alpha HayHay about some problems in his territory.

While they were busy Lijah and I were babysitting our brother and sister. It was our very first time babysitting them all alone.

I just want everything to be perfect. I was playing cars with Elliot, my little brother, on the floor. While Lijah was on the couch tickling Belle because she wouldn't say his name when he asked 'who is the strongest man in the world?' She just kept saying 'daddy' between laughter.

Suddenly we heard a loud howl from outside followed by an alarm. I've heard about this, and Alpha HayHay and daddy made us practice what to do when it happens, but it's never happened before.

The pack is under attack.

We all start making our way to the door as fast as possible. Lijah is looking out the window to see if it is safe for us to go outside to make our way to the safe room.

"Ala" We turn around to see my little brother with tears in his eyes wobbling towards us as fast as his little 2 year old legs can carry him. Lijah walk to him and pick him up while I grab Belle's hand. We will need to walk as fast as possible.

My heart is beating out of my chest. My hand is holding on to the back of Lijah's shirt as hard as I possibly can while we walk.

We get to the hardest part of our trip to the safe house. The open field. For almost a 100 meters we have to run without any cover or anything to hide behind.

When we are almost in the middle three huge wolves are standing infront of us. *Rogues*. They have ugly red and black eyes and scars everywhere. Lijah hands Elliot over to me and says "You have to run, baby girl" but I can only shake my head. I can't leave him here alone.

One of the rogues start walking closer to us licking his lips. And tears threaten to come, but I can't cry now.

Lijah starts running towards the rogues. And then something happens that leaves both me and the rogues shocked, frozen in place.

Hayden's POV:

Alpha Xavier is in my office along with all my highest rank pack members. We are discussing the current rogue problem he has been having in his territory. When we hear the pack is under attack.

I look towards Caleb and see the same worry in his eyes "The pups are home alone" I say concerned. Luckily our mates are away, having a lady's day, but that leaves the pups all alone.

I made sure Eli and Lana knows what to do in a situation like this. But practice is nothing like reality.

We make our way outside. Pack elders and women with their pups are making their way to the safe room.

"They linked from the safe room Young Alpha and Luna is not there yet." I see Alpha Xavier confused to hear that we already have a future Luna and to my side Caleb is already in wolf form.

We start walking towards them killing all the rogues we find along the way. My beta left to help the rest of the pack while we look for the pups.

It didn't take us long to find them standing in the clearing. A rogue is slowly making it's way to a scared looking Lana with the smaller ones. While two rogues are chasing after a puppy? A dog? What is that?

We are next to them in seconds killing the rogues. Caleb stands protectively infront of the pups while I turn to... not a puppy or dog, a small black wolf.

My son.

How? Impossible. He lies down and look up at me tiredly. The first shift takes a lot of energy. I make my way to him bending down petting him on the head.

"You have to shift back buddy" I say softly while a big yawn leaves his. He slowly nod his head and start shifting back.

I pull my shirt off and over his small body and pick him up in my arms. When I turned around I see Alpha Xavier with a shocked look on his face. *Don't worry man, your definitely not the only one shocked right now.*

"Caleb, I have to take Eli to the hospital we don't know the consequences of shifting this early. Bring the other pups along, they'll be safe there." He nods his head and bend down in wolf form for the three pups to get on his back.

When we get to the hospital the pack members look at me, carrying a sleeping Eli, with worry.

While the doctor is checking Eli, Alex comes up to me, telling me that the last few rogues on the pack territory just fled.

"Alpha, besides shifting at such a young age, everything is normal.

He might be tired for longer than normal wolves after shifting. His wolf must have sensed his mate being in trouble and surfaced early to protect her. Physically he will be fine after some rest." The doctor said and I nod gratefully.

Eli will be fine. He just shifted to protect his mate.

How am going to tell my mate our son shifted into his wolf. She was already emotional when he found his mate, because, and I quote, 'my little boy is growing up too fast'. She is *not* going to like this.

We take the pups home so they can rest after the long, stressful day and we call our mates to get them to come home so we can explain everything.

The pups are all upstairs when Sophia and Lila get home. We explain everything to them, the rogue attack and the shift. Tears are streaming down their faces, so we take them upstairs to show them their pups are fine.

When we get to Eli's room, we see him and Lana in bed, snuggled up together. No matter how hard we tried, they still found a way to sometimes sleep in the same bed cuddled up together so we lost hope and allow it sometimes, as long as it's not every night.

But what really caught our attention is Lana. Pieces of her black hair, turned white.

♡ ♡ ♡ ♡ ♡ ♡ ♡ ♡ ♡ ♡ ♡ ♡ ♡ ♡ ♡ ♡ ♡ ♡

Elijah had his first shift and it is way earlier than the normal wolf. Alana's hair is turning white, what is happening?

Elijah's POV:

My whole body feels heavy, I imagine this is how it feels to get hit by a truck. I'm just so tired. I slowly open my eyes to see I'm in my bed.

Not even ten seconds later my little angel comes walking through my door like she owns the place. She haven't even realized I'm awake, but as soon as her eyes land on me her mouth drops open.

She runs up to me, jumping on my already tired body, but I welcome her with open arms "You're awake" she keeps repeating like she is trying to convince herself.

I try to speak but my throat is dry and hurts. When was the last time I had something to drink? I whisper to her "thirsty" and she nods.

"I have juice for you" she picks up a juice box and shakes it a bit... empty... Throwing it to the side. She picks up another one, also empty. By the time she gets to the 5th empty juice box she looks up at my shyly.

"You were asleep for a long time" she whispers to me tears forming in her eyes, while holding a bottle of water. I guess she drank all of my juice while I was asleep and now she only has water left. *She should be glad I love her, she drank all my juice.*

I take the water from her downing half the bottle. Luckily I remember the rogue attack and me shifting into my wolf, I just had to protect my mate. "How long was I asleep for baby girl" I look up at her, a tear sliding down her face "Two days" she mumbles.

Two days? Wow. Now I look at her properly "Your hair!" a big gasp left my mouth. "Does it look bad?" I look at her taking in her black and white hair "No, you could never look bad. What happened to it?"

"I don't know, I woke up like this the day after you shifted into wolfie." I love how she calls my wolf, wolfie. 'Me agree' someone else says, who said that? how do they know what I'm thinking?

'It's me, your wolfie. We have the best mate.' I can talk to my wolf now? This is awesome.

"Why are you looking like that?" I look up at her realizing I zoned out while talking to my wolf and she has been staring at me.

"I'm talking to my wolf, I can do that now." She looks at me with a big smile "I know it's amazing! It's like having someone to talk to all the time" she says excitedly "but they can get annoying sometimes" she whispers, like that would help. And she realize it didn't help because her eyes goes wide and she covers her mouth like she just accidentally said an adult word.

"You can talk to your wolf? You shifted? When?" I asked her shocked. Why isn't she as tired as me?

She looks up at me a little ashamed. "I didn't shift, but I can talk to my wolf, I've been able to since my hair turned white, I was so confused and scared at first" she says with a frown on her face but it is instantly replaced with a smile. "She is sooo nice! Her name is Ana."

Ana? I fits her so well! Does my wolf have a name? 'Can my name be Wolfie please, please, please. That's what mate calls me, it's perfect. She is so smart to think of that name.'

Wolfie? I don't think that is a real name or appropriate for an Alpha. 'Stop being dumb, it's perfect, it's perfect! Now give mate a hug! She smells so nice, like vanilla and strawberries, my favorite.'

I internally roll my eyes at him a guess Wolfie is fine, he really likes it and my angel will like it too, but I see what she meant by they can be annoying sometimes.

Although giving my angel a hug and holding her close does not seem like a bad idea. And he is definitely my wolf because I said the same thing about her scent.

I pull her close to me holding her in my arms while we talk about our wolves, and what they are like.

Apperently her wolf made an appearance after mine so we can understand each other better and that Wolfie won't be lonely being the only wolf his age, but she can't shift yet because she's not strong and big enough it will hurt her too bad, or at least that is what her wolf told her.

After a few hours of just laying in bed talking, an idea pops into my head. "Baby girl do you think we can mind link like big wolves now?"

She looks at me with big eyes, uncertain. So I close my eyes to concentrate 'Lana baby, can you hear me?' From the gasp leaving her mouth I know she heard me and it makes me so happy, we can mind link now.

She close her eyes to concentrate as well and it didn't take me long to hear her angelic voice in my mind 'I'm happy you're awake Lijah, I missed you'

So I pull her close to me kissing her temple tiredly. How did I sleep for two days and I'm still tired. Now I think I know why the high school kids are always sleeping, I just thought they were lazy, is this how they always feel? I will have to ask daddy if I will become weird like the high school kids now.

Not long after that my momma and daddy come into my room looking tired. When they see I'm awake their face lights up and momma starts crying. Daddy says women are more emotional and we have to respect that and comfort them. But he doesn't say it in front of momma, otherwise she will smack him upside the head.

"My baby, you're awake. I'm so happy you're fine and safe. How are you feeling? Are you okay?" my momma keeps rambling on asking questions. While my daddy gives me a kiss on the forehead ruffling my hair while I hold my angel in my arms.

It didn't take long for Belle to figure out I'm awake from all the noise coming from my room. She came storming in with big eyes, running to me and giving me a big hug, refusing to let me go.

I love my family.

o o o o o o o o o o o o o o o o o o o o o o o o o o o o o o o o o o o o o o o o o o o o o o o o o o

Alana's POV

Today is Christmas Eve. We are all spending it together. We had our pack Christmas celebration last week, where all the pack members celebrate together. There was a big bon fire, and people were singing Christmas songs and eating marshmallows.

I am meeting Lijahs grandparents for the first time. They were the

45

previous Alpha and Luna, but they don't live in the pack anymore. I really hope they like me.

All of our friend and family are celebrating Christmas together this year.

Lijah and I were waiting outside for everyone to arrive when we got bored and started building a snowman. We even stole some of Aunty Li's carrots for his nose, and some rocks as buttons.

When we were done I couldn't resist saying "Hi, my name is Olaf and I love warm hugs" which resulted in Lijah picking me up in a big hug and spinning me around making me laugh uncontrollably.

As soon as he set me down on the ground, I felt something hard and cold hit my back. I turned around with a big gasp to see my daddy and all his friend *and* all my friends. *When did they all get here?*

My daddy threw me with a snow ball. I can see it from the look in his eyes, it was him! *He's going down!* This resulted in a big snow fight, pups against adults. Lijah threw himself in front of me a few times, so the snow balls would rather hit him then me.

Our battle didn't stop until we heard a car honk. All the moms were standing on the front porch. And we turned to see a few old couples next to their cars. The grandparents have arrived.

Belle tried to run up to her grandparents in excitement, but tripped and fell face first into the snow. Elliot was wobbling past her on his short legs toward our grandparents, not even giving Belle a second glance. While Lijah took my hand in his, quickly making our way to them as well.

My grandma pinched my cheeks talking in a baby voice "look how big you've gotten" I don't think she knows I'm 10 years old already and she doesn't need to do that anymore it really hurts my cheeks, but I can't say that to her, it would hurt her feelings.

When I'm done greeting my grandparents Lijah pulls my towards his grandparents with a big smile on his face "Grammy, Grand-pappa, this is Alana, my mate" they already knew Lijah found his mate so they weren't surprised but they were *way* more excited than I thought.

And apperantly they are huggers, because his grandma pulled me into a big hug 'so tight' I said to Lijah through mind link and a growl left his lips "Grammy, your squishing my mate."

He pulled me out of his grandma's embrace and held me in his arms. Then his mother hit the back of his head "No growling at your grandparents".

He just mumbled a 'sorry' rubbing the back of his head. 'With the years she just starts hitting harder and harder' he tells me through mind link and I can hear hear the disappointment in his voice, I don't even have to look at him to know he is frowning. Which results in me breaking out in a fit of laughter. Leaving his grandparents with a very confused look on their faces.

This results in me getting a slap on the shoulder by my mom "stop mind linking while in other people's company, it's rude" she scolded, making my mouth drop. It's not even my fault, he linked me!

The rest of the day was very uneventful, all of us pups played together upstairs while the adults were talking in the living room.

After dinner I felt so stuffed, I couldn't move. Why do they always have to make so much delicious food for Christmas? After dinner there was so much cake! You *can't* say no to cake. Zander had cake all over his face, the guys kept laughing at him, but he just kept eating, he could eat a whole cake by himself.

When it was time to open gifts, everyone had big smiles on their faces. Momma helped my pick out daddy's present and daddy helped to pick out momma's.

I got something of everything, toys, soapies, clothes, chocolates, flowers. Everything was so nice, but my favorite gift was from Lijah, he got me a big, big, big, teddy. It is taller than me! It is absolutely gorgeous. It was a black wolf and it reminded me of Wolfie.

I ran up to him giving him lots of kiss on his cheeks hugging him and thanking him. He is so good at giving gifts. I still wear my butterfly necklace everyday.

I just got him a black guy bracelet with a wolf and a butterfly on it, and I showed him I have a similar silver one. And I also got him his favorite basketball team jersey.

When it was getting late we went upstairs to get ready for bed, everything I need to sleep over is permanently in his room. For the amount of times I sleep over it's too much work to pack a bag every time, so I just left a few things here, if I need something I can climb through the window and get it.

When we climbed into bed I cuddled into his side, and he kissed my forehead "goodnight little angel, sleep tight" he mumbled into my hair.

"Goodnight Lijah, goodnight Wolfie." Wolfie and Ana gets jealous and sad when I don't talk to him too, and that puts me and Lijah in a bad mood, so I try to give them both attention.

I love my Lijah and Wolfie, they are the best!

We would sometimes let our wolves take over our bodies, they love spending time together. And sometimes Lijah would shift into his wolf and we would play outside together.

I never thought someone could be this happy, but here I am, over the moon!

○○○

In this chapter, Alana is 10 years old and Elijah is 11. It is the end of the year and they both had their birthdays already after the previous chapter.

I think I might have another big time jump somewhere, tell me what you think.

Chapter 6

Time jump!
Alana 15 years old and Elijah 16 years.

Elijah's POV:

Everything has been great between Alana and me. We've been cudling more than usual. Although we are very comfortable holding each other and kissing on the forehead and cheeks, we still don't kiss on the lips. We'll get there someday, she is my forever so we have all the time in the world.

My wolf gets *really* overprotective, yes you heard me right I'm blaming my wolf. No male dare look at her the wrong way or do anything that will prevoke me.

School has been great, the transition to high school wasn't even that hard, I expected it to be way worse from what people always used to say. But nothing big changed. We still do homework together, watch movies, play outside and Lana still likes to garden. **And** the best change is, my little angel can cook and bake now, and let me be the first to say, she is AMAZING! Yes, I taste *everything*.

We started combat training with Alex a few years ago. And we can already kick most of the pack warrior's butts. She has to be good because I'll hit anyone who hurts her. I also train in wolf form against them but Lana still hasn't shifted, Ana said it will happen soon. My dad and mom also started teaching us a bit about being the Alpha and Luna.

Besides me putting on some muscle, yes definitely not fat. Having to fight my mom about shaving way to often, and my voice sounding more and more like my dads', everything is great.

Or so I thought...

Now I'm sitting outside my angel's window in the rain begging her to open it up. She *kicked* me out of the house a few hours ago and I have *no* idea why.

Okay, maybe I know a little, but she is totally overreacting, her kicking me out definitely came out of nowhere.

At school today we found out about a test that we had to study for, so I told her I'll stay over tonight and we can study and watch a movie and cuddle, the whole snacks in bed deal. We love doing that. And she was happy when I suggested it.

But she was all over the place today. One second she is happy and loving, the next she is mad and if it's not that, she is crying. Happy tears, sad tears, I've seen them all today.

And then the worst happened, some stupid guy bumped into my little angel, almost causing her to fall on her pretty little butt. He broke her butterfly necklace in the process.

No one had time to react, before they knew it I was punching the guy. *How dare he bump into the future Luna, my MATE.* It is safe to say that we were asked to leave school for the rest of the day leaving my angel mad at me for punching the guy and sad about her necklace.

Have you seen someone being mad and wanting comfort from them in the same breath? It was awkward to say the least.

So we went to her house, studied in silence while I'm holding her in my arms. After a while she went to the bathroom and get us some snacks. After about half an hour she still wasn't back so I went to look for her, only to get *kicked out* by Sophia. Apperently 'Lana wants me to leave' *What?*

Now I'm soaked from head to toe. Wolfie is mad at me for getting us kicked out or 'in the dog box' as he calls it. It's getting dark, and she still won't open up. After a few more minutes Caleb climbed through my window sitting down next to me.

"How are you holding up buddy?" I look at him with pleading eyes, they can't keep me out forever. "How is she? When will she let me in? Can you please just get her to talk to me? I'll do anything"

Caleb looks at me laughing. *Laughing?* Really, he thinks this is funny. My mate is mad, my mom is gonna smack me for punching someone and he is laughing. *Unbelievable.*

"Alana is a woman now, you're going to have to get used to it." *a woman now?* Then it hits me. My mom told me this would happen, and to say that was an awkward conversation with my mom, is an understatement, and something I do not want to repeat *ever* again, but with my luck we learned about it in school too.

"So what do I do know? I can't just wait for it to past. Is it going to be this bad everytime?" I whisper the last part scared of his reply.

He burst out laughing like this is the funniest thing in the world "It is her first time so if you're lucky it will get better with time. Come on I can get you into her room, but the rest is up to you. Take snacks and drinks with you, it might help.

I take a deep breath and go back to my room changing into dry clothes and getting snacks and drinks. And going to her. As soon as she sees me in her room she runs up to me jumping into my arms wrapping her legs around my waist and her arms around my neck, just like she always does when she is excited. *I have a lot of practice catching her.*

She mumbles 'bed, movie, snacks' into my neck and there is no way I'm arguing with her. When we get in bed she lies on top of me while I'm rubbing her back.

"I'm sorry for being a meany today, I love you." I hug her tighter in my arms, now this Alana I can deal with. "I love you too little angel" I say kissing her forehead burying my face in her hair.

Let's just hope she does not kick me out every time. I am already stressed about the mood swings she will get when she is pregnant one day.

But if every mood swing ends with her in my arms I will be a lucky man. A tired, but lucky man.

○ ○

Alana's POV:4

I open my eyes, kicking my blanket down. Today is such a hot day. I turn to see I'm alone, nowadays I never know when I wake up, where I am or if I'm alone.

I sleep in his room, he sleeps in mine. He would sometimes sneak into my room when I'm already asleep because 'his *wolf* misses me', he blames poor Wolfie for everything.

I try to kick off more blankets because I'm sweating, but there is none. Ana keeps saying 'outside, find mate' but I just blow her off, I haven't even brushed my teeth I'm not going outside now.

"Where are you? Ana wants to see you." I mind link Lijah while getting up to brush my teeth. Great now I sound just like him blaming my wolf, but it's true. My whole body hurts. Maybe I'm starting to get sick.

"Hey Love, I'm with my dad, I'll come to you as soon as I can." he replies me. 'See Ana he'll come when he is...' I don't get to finish, because I drop to the floor screaming in pain.

"Help" I mind link Lijah, and soon my parents come running into my room. "*Everything hurts*" I tell them through clenched teeth.

My dad picked me up carries me outside and puts down outside on the wet grass. *Great now I'm in pain and wet. How is this helping? I need a doctor!*

"Ladybug you're shifting, don't fight the pain just let it happen." Shifting? I guess it makes sense, but why does it hurt so bad? Nobody said it was going to hurt this bad!

Another wave of pain hit me as I scream? Or howl? I don't even know but it *hurts*. Soon Lijah comes running up.

"I'm sorry, I'm here now. You're going to be okay, you're strong, you can do this" he says rubbing my back soothingly. "I can't, it hurts" I say tears coming out of my eyes as my bones start to break one at a time.

"I know, I'm sorry. It's almost over just hang on baby" he says kissing my forehead. Then everything happens so fast, I'm shifting.

When I look down, I see white paws where my feet used to be. When I look up, I see everyone with big smiles on their faces. **I did it!** I can shift now.

And I'm a white wolf, one of the rarest wolves ever! Is it wrong of me to think Wolfie and Ana looks like chess pieces together? Black and white.

"Come on Love, let's get you used to those wolf legs. We're going for a run" Lijah's voice pulls me from my thoughts that made Ana scowl.

I give Ana full control while Lijah shifts into his wolf. We run into the woods, Wolfie running behind me bitting at my tail and heels playfully.

Ana runs as fast as she can towards the water hole, wanting to test our speed. When she gets there she turns around to see Wolfie has fallen behind. So I'm a fast wolf, NICE!

I look in the water to see my reflection, white as snow. When Lijah shifted he wasn't even that interested to see how he looks because apperently all Alpha's wolves are black, but seeing my white wolf is interesting.

Out of nowhere Wolfie bites my butt. *What?* I turn around growling, how dare he? "Baby, you have a black moon imprinted on your pretty little butt" he mind links and I can hear the laughter in his voice.

He always calls it my 'pretty little butt'. But he can't bite it! We might be wolves, but we are not animals, we don't bite each other's butts.

I tackle him to the ground and we play like that for a few hours until we get tired and make our way home. When we get there I take a pair of clothes my parents left out, go behind a tree and shift back.

I go back to the house where everyone is waiting, as soon as I enter everyone is staring at me. *Yes, I just shifted, it's a big accomplishment.* A gasp leaves my moms mouth "your hair" *aww, not again!*

I look at my hair to see everything is white, no more black hair. I didn't even have time to register what is happening when someone pulls at my pants.

I turn around with big eyes pushing Lijah away "What are you doing?" He looks at me with a frown, like he was doing the most normal thing in the world and I'm the crazy one.

"You're hair is still white, I want to see of the moon is still there." he says like it should have been obvious. "go away" I say pushing him.

I pull my pants down a bit to see, I'm walking in circles like a dog trying to catch its own tail but I can't see anything. I stop when I hear Lijah snickering. "Baby, it's the other side." he laughes out while I'm glaring at him.

I turn to look and there it is. It looks like I got a tattoo of a moon on my lower back butt area. Turning around I show Lijah, and all he does is whisper 'beautiful'.

When I feel like the walking dead, Lijah helps me up to my room, putting me to bed. Luckily I won't sleep for two days like Lijah did after his shift because I'm older and stronger than he was. But right now I feel like I can sleep for a week.

Lijah climbs in next to me rubbing my back. "Your wolf is beautiful, Baby. I'm so proud of you." he tells me and I can feel my eyes getting heavy, but I don't want to fall asleep yet. I want to stay in this moment with him forever.

I didn't know it was possible, but now that I can shift, it feels like the mate bond has grown even stronger.

Alana's POV:

It is new year's eve and we are going to the annual new year's eve ball for the first time. It is one of the biggest party's of the year. All of the highest ranked Alphas of all of the packs attend it.

We bought a new dress and my mom helped me get ready.

When we made our way downstairs, my dad and Lijah were there, waiting for us. Both their eyes were huge, a soft 'wow' escaping their lips. When I made it to the last step, Lijah met me with a hug, picking me up and spinning twice before setting me down on my feet.

"Beautiful doesn't even begin to describe how perfect you look in that dress, Love" he told me, kissing me tenderly on the forehead. Then we made our way to the pack where the ball is held.

When we got there, there were cars everywhere. I don't even think our pack has a big enough venue to host a party like this.

Everything was so pretty, and everyone looked like they stepped out of a magazine. Lijah had to basically pull me not to stop at every flower or any pretty dress.

We met a few Alpha families, and made small talk here and there. You never know when you will need some allies. Omegas were walking around with food and drinks on platters.

I couldn't wait for people to start dancing. Yes, when I found out about the party I made Lijah take dance classes with me. I love dancing, and Lijah won't admit it but I know he likes it too.

It was almost midnight and 'Tuesdays by Jake Scott' was starting to play. Lijah pulled me to the dance floor, wrapping his arms tightly around my waist moving to the slow beat of the music.

As the song slowly came to an end, Lijah pulled me even closer, slowly putting his lips on mine. *We're kissing!*

The kiss is gentle and pouring with love. His lips soft against mine while butterflies and happiness burst inside me. I lock my fingers into his soft hair pulling him even closer. *How can something feel this perfect?*

His tongue slipped into my mouth, exploring. We didn't pull away until we heard people around us yelling "happy new year".

I was looking around confused, only to see people hugging their loved ones. *We're still at the party?* When I turned back to Lijah I saw him looking at me lovingly with a big smile.

"You're my Tuesday, my Everyday, my Forever. I love you so much baby, happy new year." He said softly, a happy tear escaping my eyes when I pull him down to me for another kiss. *My favorite feeling in the world.*

"I love you so much." I told him, and before I knew it, our parents were standing next to us, wishing us a happy new year. From the look in my dad's eyes I knew he definitely saw the kiss, but I just gave him a big smile and tight hug, which lifted his mood back up. *It helps to be daddy's girl.*

It wasn't long after midnight when we got home. From the look in all the parental's faces we made our way to our rooms, *separately. I guess us kissing changes things a bit for them?*

As soon as I made it into the house, my dad pulled me to his side "I can't believe you kissed that pup" he said with a disgusted look on his face while I still can't keep the smile of my face, nothing can spoil my good mood.

"No funny business in my house... Or his house... Or any house. You're still my baby. Don't grow up yet" he said with pleading eyes. I just rolled my eyes, still smiling, giving him a kiss on the cheek "g'night daddy, I love you"

"Goodnight Ladybug. Love you!" he says back happily his sour mood forgotten.

I kissed my mom on the cheek and made my way upstairs. I got ready for bed, but before I could drift off in a peaceful slumber, I felt my bed dipping to the side.

I turned around slowly only to be pulled into a warm embrace, my mate. "Wolfie missed you" he whispers into my hair making me giggle.

'Ana missed you too, Ana loves kisses, Ana loves you, Ana is so happy, Ana can stay in his arms forever, Ana can...' my wolf says happily in my head, but before she can finish her ranting I cut her off "shush you crazy wolf, it's bedtime, we're in his arms, what more do you want?"

I can practically hear her imagination going wild with all the things she wants varying from ice cream, kisses, running anything she can think of. 'Just a goodnight kiss, one goodnight kiss, a long good nice kiss, maybe a little...'

Before she can continue I leaned up and planted my lips on Lijah, he was taken by surprise but it didn't take him long to respond lovingly, curling his fingers in my hair pulling me closer.

He is definitely a better kisser then he was when he was 7 years old.

I placed my head back on his chest drifting off to sleep, but not before hearing my wolf say 'uhg... not enough.'

Early the next morning I woke up to some noises. *Too early.* I'm laying on top of Lijah his arms holding me protectively to him. I turn my head to see where all the noise is coming from, only to see my dad at my door.

Well... Not really standing at my door, more like removing my door. *What on earth?* He turn, and when he sees I'm awake he gives me a big smile and thumbs up before picking the door up and leaving my room.

Great he stole my door.

Just as I was trying to fall back asleep a ten year old Elliot comes walking into my room laying next to us on the bed whispering "you don't have a door" he was barely done with his sentence when Belle came climbing through my window as Lijah woke up giving me a lingering kiss on my neck sighing when he sees our siblings with us on the bed.

"You don't have a door. Why? Dad is busy removing Eli's door as well." Belle says and Lijah looks at her like she just told him the world is coming to an end, whispering 'parents' under his breath while shaking his head.

Looks like our parents are more stressed about this whole kissing thing than I thought. *The trust in this family.*

We spent the rest of the morning on the bed, laughing with Elliot and Belle, they are growing up way too fast. *Man, now I even sound like my mom.*

If a year starts off this good, I'm sure I'm in for a great year ahead.

o o o o o o o o o o o o o o o o o o o o o o o o o o o o o o o o o o o o o o o o o o o o o o

What do you think of that great song by Jake Scott!?

Chapter 7

Alana's POV

We are finally in our last year of high school. Lijah and I both decided we are going to a nearby college. That way, we can stay at home together and start working on alpha and Luna duties, while studying.

Lijah is going to study business management, while I'm going to study education. It will help us with our future Alpha and Luna duties.

My favorite part of the pack since I was young, was always the pupsitters, they protected me before I came to Alpha HayHay's pack and I hope that I can help some pups like they helped me.

Today it's Friday, and we are having another one of our movie nights with all our friends.

We are holding it at Lijah's house just like the first ever movie night I had with the boys. The only difference is this time all my friends are with me. I am genuinely happy.

His whole living room is filled with blankets, pillows, drinks, sweets and pizza by the time all of our friends arrive.

Like every movie night everyone argued about what to watch

first, you'd think after years of movie nights we'd have figured out a fair way to pick out a movie without arguing.

After more than ten minutes of arguing, we finally chose 'Hobbs and Shaw'. Lijah and I was cuddled up on one couch, Zander and Mila on the other, they found out the were mates, and let's just say it's been a circus. Chubbs was sitting close to the snack table, while everyone else is laying on the ground on the mountain of pillows and blankets.

Sometime during the night I fell asleep and when I wake up again I'm not sure what time it is, but it is still dark. The TV is still on, but everyone is already asleep.

It doesn't take me long to realize that the reason I woke up is because Lijah is holding me tight in his arms, rubbing his arm slowly up and down my side kissing my neck. So I slowly turn pulling his lips to my own.

When we pull away he whispers "Come on Love, let's go upstairs I want to talk to you about something" I nod and we quietly make our way to his room.

When we get there I sit down on his bed while he pace his room nervously. After a few minutes I pull him to sit down next to me "What's going on? You know if you're nervous, it makes me nervous. Talk to me." I say gently.

"I wanted it to be romantic, I planned everything. But while holding you in my arms tonight I couldn't stop thinking back to when we first met, the little angel with pitch black hair and gorgeous blue eyes. From the moment I saw you I knew you'd be mine forever and I wouldn't have it any other way." He says standing up walking to his closet to get something.

"I thought a lot about how I wanted to do this. The perfect moment, but then I realized every moment with you is perfect." He pauses showing me the most beautiful ring.

"This is a promise ring. A promise to always love and protect you. To be your shoulder to cry on and kiss your tears away. The one to experience every memorable memory with you and join in all your laughter. One day I'll replace this with a wedding ring, but for now, I hope you accept my promise ring, a promise for forever."

By the end of his speech I can't control the tears streaming down my face. I pull him into a sloppy kiss, tasting the mixture of his lips and my tears.

I pull away saying 'I love you' repeatedly between tears, while he slips the ring on my finger. I can kick half of the male wolf's butt during practice, but I can't contain my tears when my mate is being sweet. He can always bring out the best in me. He is my calm in the storm.

He pulls the covers back, deciding to stay upstairs in the bed tonight. It is a lot more comfortable than the couch. We make out for a while longer before we both fall into a peaceful sleep cuddled up together.

The next morning when we get downstairs for breakfast everyone already left. Well I guess it's not technically morning anymore, but what do you expect from us we had a late night.

When Aunty Li notice my ring she slaps Lijah on the back of the head. "Ow! What did I do now?" he asks rubbing his head with his one hand and pulling me closer to his side with the other. *Great, use me as protection to get away from your mom.*

"It was supposed to be romantic! We should have planned a date where you give it to her. You weren't supposed to give it to her last night!" She whisper yell like I'm not standing right next to Lijah and can definitely hear everything.

Then she pulls me into a hug "I'm so happy for you too." She says slapping Lijah again, and I have to bite my lip to not laugh. Lijah just gives her a look of disbelief pulling me away from her to a plate filled with breakfast. Leaving me to pour us some juice before settling back next to me.

I don't even know what my parents' reaction will be. Did they know he was gonna give me the ring? My poor dad is going to have a panic attack.

While I eat, I can't stop looking at the ring on my finger. *He definitely had some help picking it out.*

Alana's POV:

It's almost time for our final exams before we graduate. Besides from studying with me and climbing into bed next to me late at night we barely see each other.

I have no idea what keeps him this busy everyday, every time I ask him, he just gives some excuse I know is not true. Even Mila said Zander has been away a lot lately, doing something for Eli, but she doesn't know what either.

It's starting to make me worried, but every one keeps telling me to relax, and that everything will work out perfectly. I'm pretty sure my parents and his knows what is going on, but they won't tell me.

He tries not to treat me any differently, he brings me flowers cuddles with me, and talk to me about everything except what he is doing all day. But I can tell he is hiding something from me, something big.

So I decided I'm going to do what any rational teenage girl would do, I'm going to figure out what is going on!

It is weekend which means he is gone before I wake up and won't return until late when I'm already asleep. So I have all the time in the world to satisfy my curiosity. *Yes, that is it definitely not snooping or spying just satisfying my curiosity.*

So after lunch I go outside and follow his scent, it is not very hard to find his scent because firstly it is very familiar to me and hard to miss and secondly it is obvious he has been here a lot his scent is all over the place with a few other wolves, I don't even recognize all of the scents.

I was somewhere in the woods still following the scent when I heard something behind me for a second, I stood frozen thinking someone caught me. Then someone I don't recognize come out of nowhere, I start kicking and screaming, but it is no help he covers my face with something and I feel my eyes get heavy before I pass out.

A rogue

When I wake up, it takes me a few seconds to remember what happened. I don't know how long I was passed out or where I am, but my wrists hurts, being bound by wolfsbane covered ropes, burning my skin. My head hurts, probably from what ever he drugged me with.

Being in the dark room, it is hard to tell the time, does anyone know I'm kidnapped? What time is it? I don't know how long I'm alone in the dark room before the guy enter the room.

He looks so scary. He has a long scar running down his face, he is covered in tattoos. His eyes look so cold, like he has no emotions.

"Well, well, well. I have to say, you made this so easy for me. Your still just a pathetic little girl. You ruined my life, and by the time I'm done with you your going to beg me to end your life."

I stare at him, how do you even reply to something like that. I won't let him break me. "Who do you think you are? I don't know you, how did I ruin your life? They're going to find me and then you're going to be sorry." I say through clenched teeth, slightly terrified but mostly angry.

"Aw dear, how could you forget your *father*" he says in a mocking tone while my heart beat speeds up. Then he kicks me in the face, effectively knocking me out again.

Elijah's POV:

I've been so busy lately, exams are coming up, I have some alpha duties and then I am planning this big surprise for my angel.

I feel so guilty for not being able to spend as much time with her as usually, and having to lie to her about what I do everyday.

63

I know it is bothering her, but I'm almost done. Her parents, my parents, basically anyone who can keep a secret knows about what I'm doing. And everyone is willing to help me.

If everything goes as planned her surprise will be done by the time our exams begin. So that is where I am today, working on her surprise again.

Zander and a few other pack members are helping me, when I suddenly feel dizzy. "Hey man, you okay? You don't look so good." Zander says holding my arm to keep me from falling.

It didn't even last for ten seconds and I'm better that is so weird. 'Hey baby, are you okay?' I say through mind link. My parents once told me that after a couple is fully mated they can feel everything the other is feeling. Lana an I aren't fully mated, but we have an unusual strong bond and I am certain that dizzy wave did not come from me.

My mind link is not going through to her. I look up at Zander, who is still looking at me carefully "Something is wrong with Alana" I say while pushing him away to start running home with him close behind me. He knows it must be serious because I never call her by her full name.

When we get to her house, she's not there. A quickly go to my house, but she's not there either.

I mind link my parents and her parents, ready to pass out from the stress, how can she just be gone? It feels like my heart is going to explode in my chest and I can't breathe.

I didn't even realize the tears coming down my eyes until my dad pulled me into a hug "We'll find her son, you have to calm down, you can't help her in the state your in. We have trackers looking for her, we're going to find her." He whispered the last part like he is convincing himself.

We have to find her. She is my everything.⁺

"Alpha, we tracked her scent. She's been *kidnapped.*" one of the trackers tells my dad and it feels like the wind got knocked out of me.

She's been kidnapped.

Elijah's POV:

It's been more than two weeks since I've seen my little angel. I can't do anything. I'm out everyday in the woods looking for her, looking for some clue to where she can be or who took her.

I get home late at night and sleeps in her bed because it smells like her. My wolf is in his own world trying to connect with her wolf, but he still has no luck. Some people started with exams a few days ago, but there is no way I'm spending time on anything other than finding my mate.

If it weren't for my mother's treats, I wouldn't even want to waste time on eating. Finding her is my only priority.

When I get her back, there is no way I'm letting her out of my sight ever again. I was walking through the woods when I suddenly heard something in my mind 'father' it was faint, but I heard it.

I saw red as I made my way to my father's office. As soon as I enter I pin Caleb to the wall by his neck. My wolf teeth and eyes showing. It took my dad and Alex to finally get me to let go of him.

"What is wrong with you Elijah?!" my dad said the exact same time as I said "Where is she?!"

Everyone looked at me confused. "I got a faint mind link from her. She only said one word! Father" I said in a deadly tone through clenched teeth.

Everyone's faces turn pale and my dad goes behind his desk picking up his phone to make a phone call while everyone is having a conversation of their own completely ignoring me.

"Where is she!" I get everyone's attention back on me. They know something about my little angel and won't tell me.

When my dad finally ends his call he turns to talk to me "Son, she wasn't talking about Caleb. She was talking about her biological father. You never met him because we sent him to prison for abusing her, but I just called the prison where he was held and he escaped a month ago."

I knew she didn't have a good life before coming to our pack, but we never really spoke about her biological parents. Just about what she used to like.

Why couldn't I protect her?

A tear falls down my cheek when I'm suddenly hit with a terrible headache falling to my knees screaming.

I see everything she is seeing, feel everything she is feeling, I don't know how long I'm in her world before everything goes back to normal and I see everyone looking at me worriedly.

Alana's POV:

I don't know how long I've been here, but its been HELL. He doesn't give me any food, I'm starving. The only time I see water is when he is drowning me in it.

I know that if someone doesn't find me soon, I'm as good as dead. I've lost weight, even with my wolf healing I still have a lot of cuts and broken bones.

He can break my bones, but he won't break me.

Every day when he starts a beating I go into my own world, a world where everything is perfect like is used to be, where I'm safe and cuddled up in Lijah's arms. Nothing can take that away from me.

I keep trying to mind link him when I'm alone but I don't know if he is getting it. I'm so tired. I just want to close my eyes and keep the closed until everything is perfect again.

That is what I do, until the door opens and Mr Michaels walk in for another beating. I look in his hand to see his whip. This is going to be another bad one, but I just keep focusing on Lijah. It didn't take me long to pass out, either from pain, blood loss or just being to tired.

Please find me Lijah.

I wake up to a beeping sound, *great he got me a alarm for this dark hell he keeps me in.* When I try to open my eyes they won't open the first time, but after a few attempts they open revealing white.

Everything is white.

I'm alone in a hospital room. Someone rescued me. I stand up with shaky legs everything hurts, but I've been through worse most of my wounds look like they already started healing. *How long have I been here?*

I start making my way out of my hospital room but no one is paying me any attention, where is Lijah and my family. I try to catch their scent, but everything smells like hospital.

"I'm sorry, she is healing like she is supposed to, but she went through a lot of trauma, I can't say when or if she is going to wake up. Only time will tell" I hear someone say.

"If?! What do you mean if?! She has to wake up!" Lijah! That is his voice! I follow it as fast as my tired legs will carry me until I bump into someone.

Elliot

He looks at me with big eyes a tear rolling down his eye. "you're awake" he whispers and I pull him into a tight hug "Hey baby brother, I missed you so much."

"I missed you too so much, I stole one of your teddies. I'm a big boy I don't sleep with teddies anymore, but it reminded me of you." he says while I wipe his tears away smiling at my not so little brother.

"Mom" my brother tries to catch her attention. "Not now Elliot. This insane doctor doesn't know how to do his job he says your sissy might never wake up."She says not even glancing our way.

Everyone continue arguing with the poor doctor while my brother just rolls his eyes. It might not be the right time but a laugh escapes my lips.

It's great to be back home!

Everyone is silent instantly when they hear my laugh. Turning to me slowly. Lijah runs up pulling me into a tight hug, kissing me anywhere his lips can reach in this close proximity.

My parents break down in tears and everyone comes in for a big family hug.

Apparently I was in a coma for a week and a half. But I'm awake now and safe and I am not leaving my people again.

o o o o o o o o o o o o o o o o o o o o o o o o o o o o o o o o o o o o o o o o o o o o o o

Chapter 8

Alana's POV:

Turns out I was in a coma for a whole week. I was pretty beaten up when they found me. Mr Michaels wasn't the only rogue who escaped, but they found all of the prisoners at the same place I was being held.

It was a miracle I survived, apparently some of those people were even more dangerous than Mr Michaels.

Apparently everyone is already half way through their exams, except Lijah and I. But Alpha HayHay said they would make an exception for us and still let us write so we don't have to redo the year. *It is nice to know people with authority.*

I was shocked when they told me Lijah could see through my eyes and some of my memories. That is the only reason they found me.

Everyone else was just shocked in general. They have heard of mates feeling the other's pain and sometimes emotions, but they have never heard of mates seeing through each other's eyes and into their memories.

I have no idea why it happened but I'm am so glad it did. Maybe it is because of our mate bond?

I was so happy to be back with my family. Once my mom finally stopped crying everyone sat in my hospital room just talking, joking around and having a nice time.

The doctors said I had to spend another night in the hospital although my wounds is healing pretty good, but I have to stay just to be safe.

Lijah sent everyone home, saying he would stay with me. I debated on scolding him or ignoring him or saying something about the way he treated me before I got kidnapped, but I didn't.

He looked so tired and like he lost weight and he already had an guilty, sad look in his eyes, I didn't want to throw salt in the wound. I don't even care about it anymore I just want to be back in his arms, safe.

He spent that whole night in an uncomfortable chair next to my hospital bed, sleeping with his head on my tummy and his arms circled around my waist like he is scared I'm going to dissappear. And that is how I fell asleep, scared of having nightmares.

I was standing in a green field, filled with daisies. Looking around, everything seemed so unfamiliar.

"Hello dear, I thought it best we talked in a place you would like." I turned to see a beautiful woman in a short white flowy dress. Although I didn't know her she seemed like an old friend.

She must have seen the confusion on my face because she continued "You don't know me personally, but you know me. I'm the moon goddess. I thought it best not to visit you while in your coma because you needed your rest to heal, but I think you also need answers."

I looked at her in confusion and amazement. The moon goddess is standing right in front of me.

"You see, you and Elijah are in a manner, very special to me, that is why I made you realize you are mates so early, that is why I made your bond so strong. So you can alway protect each other, so nothing can come between you. That is why I marked you both after you shifted for the first time"

Marked us? Does she mean the moon on my butt? Lijah never said anything about him having a moon on his butt.

She saw more confusion and continued with a small chuckle "Dear, he has it in the back of his neck if you check closely."

I nodded in understanding. What it's not like I went searching for a moon tattoo on his body before. So I've never seen it, it's not a big deal, right?

"A war is coming, and your future children will be the saviors of all werewolves. They will be werewolf royalty and each have different powers of their own. Raise them to become leaders, and be the good parents that I know in your hearts you could be."

That left me even more shocked, but all I did was nod. She bent down picked a daisy and handed it to me giving me a soft kiss on the cheek before dissappearing.

Waking up I was shocked from my dream, but I knew it wasn't just a dream. *I met the moon goddess and I didn't even say a word to her not even a peep. What is wrong with me?*

Looking down I saw Lijah still sleeping in my tummy. I look on his neck and sure enough, there it is, a moon just like mine, just a bit smaller.

My touch on his neck brought him out of his sleep. He gave me a tired grin "Your still here".

I nodded telling him I'm never leaving him again, also telling him about my encounter with the moon goddess. Leaving him with tons of (stupid) questions 'how many kids will we have? who will they look like? how does my tattoo look?'

I tell him I met the *moon goddess* and that's his questions, unbelievable. I'm just hoping they will all be safe. Okay fine! I'm a bit curious about how many kids we will have, hopefully two, three at most.

We spent the rest of the night/early morning just talking until I can get released, neither of us feeling too tired. Just happy to be back together.

○○○

Alana's POV:

Walking through the woods blindfold is much harder than I would have thought. Even with Lijah leading me and my wolf senses, I keep tripping over rocks and sticks.

I love the man but he is *way* too excited to lead a blindfolded person, he forgets I'm blindfolded and keeps pulling me to walk faster.

I am finally allowed to see what he has been doing with all his time. "Okay, we're here, you can take the blindfold off!" he says excitedly.

I look at the beautiful house in front of me, when I turn to Lijah I see him holding his breath.

"It's pretty. I didn't know there was a house in this part of the pack. Who lives here?" I say taking in my surroundings. I thought all of the houses were on the other side of the pack house.

When I look back at Lijah I see his excited mood gone, and he has a frown on his face. "We do, or we will. That is what I've been doing, I wanted to surprise you."

I look back to the house a big gasp escaping my lips. He had this beautiful house build for us? Before he could do anything I jumped into his arms hugging him, effectively making us both fall to the ground. *You'd think he'd be better at catching me after 12 years.*

Apparently my mate is *rich*. Okay fine, he is not rich but he will be. This was partly a loan from his father and partly from the pack that puts money aside to build a house for their Alpha and Luna- . *So most of the pack knew about my surprise!*

Apparently Alpha HayHay isn't only an Alpha but also owns a few human businesses, and that is where most of the money comes from and one day Lijah will take over those businesses as well.

Apparently there are a few people that has jobs outside the pack for extra money. I didn't know that. I guess that is why some people are so rich.

We went into the house, him showing me all of the different rooms. The whole house is already furnished but not decorated, he said he wanted us to do it together.

Together? Funny! We both know I'm doing most of the decorating. He sucks at it. He can make sure everything I get is hanging straight on the wall or something.

We are standing in the living room, my arms around his neck, his around my waist "This is the best surprise ever. I love you." I say playing gently with his hair.

"Can we get a puppy?" I kiss his forehead.

"No"

"Can we get a puppy?" I kiss his nose.

"No"

"Can we get a puppy?" I kiss his left cheek.

"No"
This 'no' was definitely more strained. I'm totally winning him over. We're getting a puppy!

"Can we get a puppy?" I kiss his right cheek.

"N-No"

"Will you mark me?" I peck his lips.

"N... Wait what?" he says with big eyes.

"I asked if we could get a puppy." His big eyes turn into a frown. "No you didn't you asked if..." He stops mid sentence in confusion, thinking maybe his brain is playing tricks on him.

"Will you mark me" his eyes turned big. "You did say that! Are you sure you want me too?" he asks barely containing his excitement.

Now it's my turn to look at him like he is dumb "Lijah, we've known we are mates since I was five, I've shifted for the first time a year, almost two years ago. There are fully mated wolves our age already expecting pups, I don't care that we aren't that far yet, but I really want you to mark me."

He looks at me with a big smile pulling me into a kiss, his tongue exploring my mouth before he pulls away kissing down my neck in search of the right place.

I bend my neck to the side giving him more access, when a small moan comes from my body he knows he found the place.

His wolf teeth extends, giving me one last kiss before he claims me. Pain burns through my whole body for a few seconds before it turns into pleasure like I've never felt before.

That night we got fully mated. Just like the marking, I felt pain first and then it was unimaginable pleasure.25

When I woke up the next morning we were both still naked, me sleeping on top of him.

I lifted my head to look at him, he looked so handsome and peaceful. When my eyes connect with his neck a big gasp escape my lips, effectively waking him up.

I marked him. When did I mark him? Does he know I marked him? Females don't usually mark male wolves. How am I supposed to tell him I marked him?

"Baby, it's okay I know you marked me. I'm happy you did. I love you." he says with a little chuckle.

"Your fine with i... How did you know what I was thinking?" Realization hit me and I look at him with big eyes.

He just shrugs "I don't know I just heard you like you were talking to me, like through mind link, but somehow I knew you weren't mind linking me." he says tiredly like it's the most normal thing in the world.

He can read my mind! What if I think something I don't want him to know? This is bad! I can never surprise him again in my life.

"Baby, relax, I'm sure if you concentrate you would be able to block me out, just like you can do with mind link" he says with a small grin.

I concentrate on blocking him out like he said. 'Why did I have to tell her she can block me out. Stupid, stupid, stupid. I like hearing what she thinks, she is so cute and adorible and my mate. My amazing mate. She looks so pretty this morning. Who am I kidding she looks pretty every morning. How can someo...'

He didn't get to finish his thoughts because I couldn't contain my laughter any longer. "Aww man, you can read my mind too?"

All I can do is nod with a big smile on my face. He is right it feels great to hear what is going on in your mate's head.

"Please just forget you heard any of that." he says with big pleading eyes.

My only response is pulling him down for a kiss. I don't even care about morning breath, if we are not used to it by now we never will be, and we are going to be waking up next to each other for a long, long time.

We finally pull away "We can get the damn puppy" he says irritated before pulling me back into a kiss.5

I'm guessing we're not getting out of bed any time soon.

o o o o o o o o o o o o o o o o o o o o o o o o o o o o o o o o o o o o o o o o o o o o o o o

When she says puppy she is talking about an actual dog. When she says pups or pup she is talking about kids.

Elijah's POV:

Around lunch time we finally get up and go back to our parent's house. I would never be able to call this my home again after spending a wonderful night with my beautiful mate at our new home.

Walking in there is no way to hide our *activities* from last night from anyone. Everyone seems genuinely happy for us, even Caleb, I can see it in his eyes, even if he tries to give me the tough dad look.

Belle and Elliot just smells our new combined scent, giving us a look I don't even know how to describe, before minding their own business. *I think they might be going through a phase.*

"We wanted you to wait until after graduating high school before getting fully mated, but we expected it to happen a long time ago, so I guess we have to be happy with what we got" Caleb tells us digging into the food in front of him.

"I would be lying if I said I didn't expect it, that is why I started planning your Alpha and Luna ceremony." My dad says like it's nothing.

I look at my little angel in my arms gulping down the nothingness or nerves in my throat. "The Alpha and Luna ceremony usually counts as a wedding as well" I say looking at the parentals.

They just look at me like I said the most obvious thing in the world, nodding their heads.

"Yep next month." My dad says continuing eating. *How can they be so.. so.. unbothered about this.* It's not like we're talking about taking over a pack and getting married *note the sarcasm*.

"Aw son, we knew this was coming since you were six, stop looking at us like that, and acting like it is new news to you. We will still be helping out with the pack and the business until you graduate college and is ready to take over. But an Alpha pair gets introduced to the pack after they are fully mated, you knew this."

Lana looks up at me searching for something in my eyes after my dad's words. All I can do is give her a reassuring nod. I always knew I would marry her, I just always thought it will happen after I properly proposed. Now it is happening in a month.

Time jump!
A month later.

Living the last month with my beautiful mate has been amazing. She is so indecisive when it comes to the damn puppy I promised her, so we still haven't gotten one. Deep down I'm glad we haven't, but I'm not telling her that, she is searching everywhere for 'the perfect puppy'. 'Cute and fluffy' she said. I thought all puppies are cute and fluffy to girls, like all babies are adorable to girls.

She has been acting a bit strange the past week, but I think it is just because she is stressed about today's ceremony.

I'm standing on a small stage in front of our whole pack, our whole family. Even our grandparents came for the celebration.

Nervous. Stressed. A bit terrified. Those are all the emotions running through my body. I don't even know if it's my feelings or my little angel's. I don't know why I feel them, deep down I'm all giddy and excited, but I can let those emotions out before I don't have my beautiful mate standing next to me.

Than I see her. It knocks the wind right out my lungs. My wolf is howling in my head in joy. I am the luckiest man on earth. She is the love of my life, she is all mine.

The dress fits like a glove. I can see the worry and excitement in her eyes. Caleb is leading her to the small stage. Taking her hand in mine I link her arm in mine holding her close to me listening to my dad start the ceremony.

Okay maybe I'm not listening to my dad, because I don't know how long I've been staring at my gorgeous mate when she squeezes my arm to bring me back to reality.

My dad gives my a knowing look before continuing or maybe repeating what he said.

"Elijah repeat after me. I Elijah Grey Stevens, take you, Alana Hale to be my Luna and wife. To protect and cherish. Through good times and bad times. Through sickness and health, for as long as we both shall live."

I repeat my fathers words and mouth 'I love you' to her. Then it's her turn to repeat everything my father says, to which I loose all my concentration again. *How can someone be that beautiful?*

When she is done it is time for the exchange of wedding rings. Not all wolves do this part since we already marked each other, but I want everyone to know she belongs to me, werewolf and human. After she slides my black wedding band on my finger I surprise her by pulling a different ring out of my pocket to replace her promise ring.

I really hope it fits. It used to be my grandmother's ring and there wasn't any time for me to resize it.

When I slide the ring on her finger a big gasp left het mouth as tears pool in her eyes. *That has been happening a lot lately too.*

After the rings, they brought an ancient knive and bowl, we each made a small cut on our hands, after I gave my angel a reassuring nod that it won't hurt too bad.

With that our blood bond with our pack formed. I could practically feel the bond between myself and my pack grow stronger. And I could feel the power that comes with the Alpha title, now that it is mine.

With all of the official ceremony business behind our backs, I pulled my angel closer, crashing my lips onto hers. I could hear clapping from the crowd but I couldn't cut the kiss short. She is like a drug, juice is nothing compared to the taste of her lips, I'm addicted.

When we pulled away to get some air, tears were streaming down her face. She mumbled something under her breath that I couldn't quite hear.

"What's that Baby, I can't hear you" I said gently wiping her tears away. It was probably just something like 'I love you', but I can never hear her say that enough so I want her to repeat it.

She looks me in the eye and whispers "I'm pregnant"[11]

And that is how I fainted. In my first ten minutes of being an Alpha. In front of my whole pack. Just great!

o o o o o o o o o o o o o o o o o o o o o o o o o o o o o o o o o o o o o o o o o o o o o o o o o o

Chapter 9

Lijah's POV:

If I can survive my mate being pregnant I can survive *anything*. After finding out she is pregnant and I fainted she cried for two days straight because she said I didn't want the baby.

Looking back I have no idea how I didn't see it before. I just taught she was having a bad period again, but *man* was I wrong!

I am thanking my lucky stars werewolf pregnancies only lasts six months. She already started showing and I tried every answer to the question she just loved to ask 'Lijah do you think I look fat?' Anything I tried ended with her crying her eyes out and me cuddling her for the whole day.

By now I'm sure she only cries because she likes my amazing cuddles. But I finally got an answer that got me in a safe place and *everyone* else at hell's door "Baby, I'm biased, I love you too much, to me you always look perfect, you are going to have to ask someone else"

And let us not even begin with her weird cravings. Peanut butter and anything. She eats everything with peanut butter. Peanut butter and fries. Peanut butter and corrots.

Once she was craving popcorn and peanut butter in the middle of the night, but we didn't have popcorn so I went knocking on every door in the pack looking for popcorn. By the time I got back she was sleeping. Climbing in bed she woke up crying because I wasn't in bed cuddling her, rubbing her back soothingly I told her "Baby, it's okay I'm back now, I was just looking for some popcorn for you."

Can you guess what her response was. "Aww, where is my popcorn?"

Other than that everything was perfect, we talked about our future, cuddled, talked about baby names, cuddled, went to work, cuddled, ate, cuddled, ate, cuddled, got the nursery ready, cuddled, stressed about raising a baby, cuddled, spent time with our family, cuddled.

It was a few weeks before her due date, and I was calm as a cucumber. She made sure everything was perfect, her bags was already packed and we were ready for anything.

Alana's POV:

It is a few weeks before the baby was due and I think we are ready. Lijah has been the best through this pregnancy. Not once complaining about my mood swings or weird cravings.

He even tried and liked some of the things I craved. Like popcorn and peanut butter. He refuses to try the peanut butter and pasta, but I think he'd like it.

He comforts me and give me hope that we will be amazing parents. He never made me feel uncomfortable about my new pregnant body, saying that he loves every inch of me.

When my tummy got to big to fit into my own clothes he let me borrow his t-shirts and sweatpants.

He got even more overprotective, never wanting to leave me alone, always tracking me with his eyes when I move to make sure I don't fall. Never leaving me alone in the house in case something happens.

Tonight we are just staying in, watching a movie and eating pizza and peanut butter snacks and drinking juice.

We are watching 'The longest ride', he let me pick the movie. I stood up to leave because I needed the bathroom when my water broke.

"Lijah, the baby is coming" he leaned forward on the couch taking another slice of pizza out of the box.

"I know baby, next week. We'll be ready" he says casually. "No Lijah, I mean my water just broke the baby is coming now"

He looks at me, all the color draining from his face, dropping his pizza. "No, the baby can't be coming, we have another week to prepair." he says, panicking.

"Lijah Love, we got to get to the hospital now" he looks at me nodding mumbling to himself 'get to the hospital, get to the hospital' he kept repeating.

He got the car keys and our bags and start making his way to the car and driving to the hospital.

Another little contraction came and I put my hand on my tummy "Baby, how long do you think it's going to take your daddy to realize we're not in the car with him"

I was about to call someone to help when I saw the car pulling back into the driveway. He climbed out and gave me a guilty look "I think I forgot something" he said shyly making his way over to me. I just gave him the 'you think' look while he helped me into the car.

A few hours later

"I hate you! I hate you so much!" I hold onto my tummy. He wipes the sweat off my forehead "I know baby, I know. It's almost over. You have to start pushing."

"I can't I'm too tired. Please don't make me. If you love me you won't make me push." He sighs wiping more sweat away "I'm not making you Baby, our baby in you tummy is. You have to push"

"There is no way I'm ever letting you put another baby in me!" He gives me a guilty look and I start pushing.

After a while I hear the most beautiful sound in the world. My baby is crying. That was the worst pain I ever felt but it was forgotten with just one sound. *My baby crying.*

"It's a boy!" Were having a boy! The doctor takes him to the side cleaning him up before coming back to me and giving me my baby boy.

He already has chocolate brown hair like his daddy. He is the most precious thing I've ever seen in this world. Lijah leans down giving me a kiss. "Okay, you win, I want many more babies, and I definitely do not hate you. I love you so so much."

He gives me a big smile leaning further down giving our boy a kiss on the forehead. When he is done I do the same.

"Welcome to the world Xavier Cole Stevens"

5 years later

Alana's POV:

"Lijah, kids! People are arriving for the party." I yelled trying to get everyone to come outside. Lijah had to go back up to change the kids' clothes because the made a mess of themselves.

Xavier was the first to come running outside "Momma, it's my birthday!" he yells running around, making me regret giving him a birthday treat this early in the morning.

He could be very responsible for his age most of the time, but he is a kid and likes to have his fun.

I am supposed to take it slow because I am pregnant again! But I've been through this three times before and I was fine, this time can't be too different.

I told Lijah this was the last one, no more. If he gets me pregnant again, he is sleeping on the couch for the rest of his life.

"Unc Elt!" My two year old son wiggles out of my mate's embrace trying to get to his favorite uncle. Elliot was only 17 but he was already one of the best warriors. Chace wobbles over to Elliot and luckily Elliot reaches the little daredevil before he falls face first down the porch steps.

I would not be lying if I said, that little two year old does not have an ounce of fear in his little body.

Lijah comes to stand behind me and wraps his arm that is not holding our daughter around me, holding my huge baby bump.

Malia is daddy's little girl, if the three year old girl isn't making sure her two brothers stay out of trouble she is with her daddy.

She is always trying to make sure everyone is safe and protected. Ever at three years old she is a little mother henn in her own way. Kissing the boys' boo boo's when the fell and hurt themselves.

She will definitely not like it when the new addition to our family makes her arrival, because then she won't be the only girl any-more.

While Xavier has chocolate brown hair like Lijah. The other two has pitch black hair like I did before it turned white. Chace has green eyes like his daddy and Xavier has my blue eyes, while Malia has Grey eyes. I have no idea where she gets those, but they are so pretty.

We have our ups and downs. Our morning tantrums. The hard days I just want to stay in bed cuddled up with my handsome mate.

Luckily our good days a thousand times more than the bad ones. Waking up next to all my smiling kids. Playing in the garden. Movie nights with all our friends. Chasing our dreams.

I can honestly say, I am proud of the person I have become and I am proud to call Lijah my mate.

He is still as innocently romantic and caring as the first day I saw him.

And the most amazing thing is seeing the little parts of Lijah and I mixed together in our perfectly imperfect kids.

Seeing them grow and learn everyday.

° °

Made in United States
Orlando, FL
19 July 2025

63101408R00051